Views from an Empty Nest

To Warren & Bari,
It's fun to share my "tales" with you!
Best wishes—
Madelyn F. Young
4/28/14

Views from an Empty Nest

Award-Winning Tales Written after Fifty

Madelyn F. Young

iUniverse, Inc.
Bloomington

Views from an Empty Nest
Award-Winning Tales Written after Fifty

Copyright © 2012 by Madelyn F. Young

All rights reserved. No part of this book may be used or reproduced by any means, graphic, electronic, or mechanical, including photocopying, recording, taping or by any information storage retrieval system without the written permission of the publisher except in the case of brief quotations embodied in critical articles and reviews.

This is a work of fiction. All of the characters, names, incidents, organizations, and dialogue in this novel are either the products of the author's imagination or are used fictitiously.

iUniverse books may be ordered through booksellers or by contacting:

iUniverse
1663 Liberty Drive
Bloomington, IN 47403
www.iuniverse.com
1-800-Authors (1-800-288-4677)

Because of the dynamic nature of the Internet, any web addresses or links contained in this book may have changed since publication and may no longer be valid. The views expressed in this work are solely those of the author and do not necessarily reflect the views of the publisher, and the publisher hereby disclaims any responsibility for them.

Any people depicted in stock imagery provided by Thinkstock are models, and such images are being used for illustrative purposes only.

Certain stock imagery © Thinkstock.

ISBN: 978-1-4697-6152-7 (sc)
ISBN: 978-1-4697-6154-1 (hc)
ISBN: 978-1-4697-6153-4 (e)

Printed in the United States of America

iUniverse rev. date: 02/28/2012

This first published work is dedicated to my family, especially my husband, Robin, and my children, Steve, Marty, and Sharon, who have lovingly supported my creative efforts for many years.

Contents

Acknowledgments xi
Introduction xiii

FICTION

Nature's Gift 3
    Author's note 8
Lost and Found 9
    Author's Note 14
The Letter Writer 15
    Author's Note 18
A Broken House 19
    Author's Note 23
Best Laid Plans 24
    Author's Note 28
Behind Closed Doors 29
    Author's Note 35
Death Comes Walking 36
    Author's Note 41
The Other Side of the Bed 42
    Author's Note 47
Encounter 48
    Author's Note 53

Chigger Lessons 54
   Author's Note 57

Amanda's Secret. 58
   Author's Note 62

Ghost Story. 63
   Author's Note 68

The Lion's Den 69
   Author's Note 75

Happy Thanksgiving, Son 76
   Author's Note 80

Unexpected Gifts. 81
   Author's Note 85

A Hundred Thousand Times Better. 86
   Author's Note 91

Petty Crime. 92
   Author's Note 93

Glory Treasures 94
   Author's Note 99

The Woman in 613 100
   Author's Note 103

Priceless. 104
   Author's Note 109

NONFICTION

The Surprise 113
   Author's Note 115

The Playhouse. 116
   Author's Note 119

Good Intentions 120
    Author's Note 124

The Perfect Pea 125
    Author's Note 127

Borderline 128
    Author's Note 131

Conversion 132
    Author's Note 136

Soft Beds 137
    Author's Note 139

Deliver Us from Evil 140
    Author's Note 143

My Life with a Loving Atheist 144
    Author's Note 147

A Thanksgiving to Remember 148
    Author's Note 151

Uncle Sam Greets Little Sam 152
    Author's Note 155

Acknowledgments

I am indebted to many writers who have guided me through the finer points of storytelling and have encouraged me with their feedback:

Current and former members of Village Writers' Club Critique Group: John Achor, Joyce Anderson, Linda Black, Jerry Davis, Nancy Foris, Marcia Greathouse, Janet Holt, Mickey Jordan, and Mary Lou Moran;

Members of Tuesday Critique Group: Judy Carroll, Elizabeth Foster, Linda Hamon, Gene Heath, and Mary Ann Robertson;

Current and former members of Arkansas Online Critique Group: Jim Barton, Sara Gipson, Amy Gray Light, Mike McMinn, Steve Whisnant, Ellen Withers, and Pam Withroder.

A special word of thanks goes to my talented friend Judith Waller Carroll of Hot Springs Village, Arkansas, who critiqued and edited the final draft.

Introduction

When a woman enters her seventies, it's time to quit talking about what she's going to do and get on with it—either fish or cut bait, as the old saying goes. I've been writing my stories, essays, and memoirs for a while now. If I want to deliver them to my children and grandchildren before I'm gone, now's the time to pull them into a book. Of course, I hope a few others will enjoy these tales too—especially friends and fellow writers who have encouraged me in this pursuit.

Views from an Empty Nest: Award-Winning Tales Written after Fifty includes what I consider a cross-section of my best work. After our children left home, writing became a favorite pastime. However, most pieces in this collection are products of my retirement years in Hot Springs Village, Arkansas. Here I have enjoyed active membership in the Village Writers' Club, and my critique group partners have helped me hone my skills. It's been fun to win writing awards along the way as well.

For the most part, these stories are clean, adult tales. However, with apologies to family and members of my church, Presbyterian Kirk in the Pines, I do reserve the right to use a curse word at times, if that's what a character would say. And a few stories deal with what I call "gritty" subjects. I hope my readers will understand and accept these pieces as reflections of life.

Mostly, I hope my five grandchildren and their children will look back one day and think it cool that their Maddie penned a book.

Madelyn F. Young
Summer 2011

FICTION

Nature's Gift

The old man shifted in the straight-backed chair, reached inside his collar, and ran calloused fingers across the back of his neck.

Dadgum tags! The things were itching him to death. He should have cut them out before he left.

The door to the office opened, and the mayor's secretary smiled. "You may come in now, Mr. Whitaker."

He rose, made his way past the woman, and entered the meeting room. The mayor, seated at the head of a long table, stood to welcome him.

"Come in, come in, Jeremiah. All these folks are eager to meet you. Gentlemen, this is Jeremiah Whitaker, the best hunting and fishing guide you'll find anywhere in Arkansas."

Jeremiah surveyed the group assembled around the table. Several wore glasses and looked like professors. He stood there waiting.

The mayor continued. "Come on over here and have a seat." He motioned to an empty chair near the far end of the table. "Jeremiah here knows the Cache River Basin like the back of his hand. He'll be a great asset to your team."

Jeremiah pulled out the chair and settled down. He looked up and cleared his throat. "I reckon I've been on the river now for forty years or more. Seen lots of fellers try their hand at reapin' the river's rewards. Plenty of ducks, geese, fish, even an ol' 'gator or two have been collected out there."

"Well, this excursion will be a bit different, my friend." The mayor gestured toward the others. "These fellows are here to spot a very special bird—the ivory-billed woodpecker. Everyone thought the bird was extinct—one hasn't been seen in sixty years. But a few weeks ago a kayaker from Hot Springs reported on a canoe club website that he saw the bird while he was out in the Cache River National Wildlife Refuge."

The mayor paused, sipped water from a glass, and then continued. "At first this guy wasn't real sure if he'd actually seen an ivory-billed. Thought it might have been just a large pileated woodpecker. They're about the same—both have that red top-knot, only the ivory-billed has more white on the top of its wings. It's larger, and it has that white beak, of course. But he was pretty excited about it."

"Mr. Whitaker, we're here to verify the sighting." The man seated directly across from Jeremiah adjusted his glasses. "My name is James Simmons. My colleagues and I are from Cornell University Department of Ornithology. Before we announce to the world this rare bird is alive and well, we need to make sure. We're putting together a research team, and we'd like you to guide us into the bird's habitat. All of this is under wraps right now, though, so we won't have a thousand birders swarming in here to catch a glimpse. You understand, you'll be sworn to secrecy."

Jeremiah's sharp eyes squinted at the man. "Well, I reckon I can lead you anywhere you want to go, but I'll need some pay for my time."

"Of course." The man nodded. "We understand that. The university is financing this expedition, and you'll be well compensated. But we need your expertise to navigate through the refuge."

"I 'preciate your kindness, Mr. Simmons. Me and my grandson, Will, live back down in the river bottom. We don't get nothin' but welfare and food stamps most of the year—at least til duck huntin' season opens. Then I get a little bit from the big city fellers who come in here. The boy goes to school, though, and he needs clothes and all. Your pay will help us out."

"Then it looks like we've got a deal." Mr. Simmons rose and extended his hand across the table.

Jeremiah stood and grasped it firmly. "Yessir, I'll be glad to help. Just let me know when."

"Great! We'll get started in the morning. Let me introduce you to the rest of these gentlemen."

Mr. Simmons recited the names and occupations of the others, and

Jeremiah acknowledged each with a nod. This was going to be some kind of a trip, but for the right kind of money, he'd do whatever these Yankees wanted—even try to find some crazy ol' woodpecker. Man! Some folks was weird.

Chuckling to himself, Jeremiah left the office, climbed into his truck, and headed toward home.

◆ ◆ ◆

Down the gravel road the yellow school bus rumbled along and screeched to a halt. Clouds of dust billowed as Will swung down the front steps onto the ground and turned to wave as the driver proceeded on his way. He trotted across the bare yard, bounded onto the porch, threw open the door, and tossed his books on the kitchen table.

Grandpa's pick-up wasn't parked under the tree out front. He'd be back before supper, though. Will looked at the clock. Only four. There would still be a couple hours before the sun went down.

Will grabbed cookies from the package on the counter, picked up his rifle, and made his way down to the dock behind the house.

The Cache River offered great adventure for a ten-year-old boy. Paths of murky water undulated through miles of swampy underbrush where bald cypress, tupelo, and oak stood silhouetted against the horizon. Many kinds of water-fowl, birds, and other wildlife inhabited the river basin. The boy rowed his boat under overhanging branches, keeping a watchful eye for water moccasins and alligators.

It was peaceful out here on the river. The hum of insects droned around him. Occasionally, he would see a beaver slip off the bank into the water. Fish wriggled up to investigate the boat's hull and then darted away.

In the distance Will could hear a steady drumming of something. Rap-rap. Rap-rap. Rap-rap. Rap-rap. His boat drifted toward the sound. Must be an ol' pecker-wood. He lifted his hand to shield his eyes.

High in the tree the large black-and-white bird busily worked. The bright red crest on its head shone in the afternoon's light. That sapsucker was huge! Two feet long, at least. The bird flipped pieces of bark left and right, left and right as it scooted around on all sides of the tree. Its ivory beak glistened as it hammered the dead trunk. In the boat below, Will didn't move.

◆ ◆ ◆

It was getting late by the time Jeremiah pulled his truck into the yard and turned off the ignition. He entered the kitchen. Books scattered on the table told him the boy had come and gone. Outside, he looked to see if the boat was at the dock. It wasn't.

A gunshot rang out. Jeremiah shook his head. Every afternoon that boy could hardly wait to get out and shoot that new gun of his. Probably killed another snake or a turtle.

◆ ◆ ◆

On the river Will laid his rifle down and took a deep breath. He'd done it. Then he turned the boat around and headed for home. Grandpa wouldn't believe what he had killed today.

Thirty minutes later he maneuvered the boat next to the dock, threw the rope around the post, and pulled in close. He stepped out and scurried up the bank.

The back door slammed. "Grandpa, I'm home."

"Figured you was out huntin' again." Grandpa smiled as he peeled taters at the sink. "Heard that gun of yours."

"Yeah! When I was down about a mile from here, I spotted this huge bird—a big black-and-white woodpecker. He was really goin' to town, tearin' up a big ol' hick'ry."

"Whoa." Grandpa spun around and glared at Will. "You didn't shoot him, did you?"

Will shook his head. "Nah, Grandpa, I wouldn't do that." Then he ducked his head and grinned. "But while I was watchin' him, this ol' bobcat was watchin' him too. I saw the cat ready to pounce, so I took aim, and I got him. Pow! Right in the neck. He fell off the limb, and that was the last I saw of him. I couldn't believe I got him with one shot."

Grandpa threw back his head and cackled. "Dang it, boy. You're gettin' to be a real sharp-shooter." He paused. "But no matter what those fellers said, I think I'd better tell you where I was today. Nature's done given us a gift, and today you was on her side, but tomorrow might be a diff'rent story."

Will frowned.

"Don't you worry none, though. You're a good boy, Wilson Whitaker." Grandpa pulled Will close and gave him a hug. "I'm proud of you, boy. Yessir, right proud."

Smiling, Will wrapped his arms around the old man's waist. He pressed his face into Grandpa's new shirt. It smelled good—real good.

Author's note: NATURE'S GIFT

This fictional story is based on the actual rediscovery of the ivory-billed woodpecker in eastern Arkansas early in 2004. Fascinated by all the excitement surrounding the event, I collected news clippings for weeks. Then I created this tale.

"Nature's Gift" won first place in the Margaret Ponder Thompson Award at Arkansas Writers' Conference in June 2006. The contest called for "prose with an Arkansas setting." Later that year it was published in *The Storyteller* magazine in the October/November/December edition.

Readers of *The Storyteller* also voted for their favorite stories in that issue. I was thrilled when "Nature's Gift" won the second place People's Choice Award for Fiction.

Lost and Found

Even though she was retired, Marian was determined to stay fit. Her early morning walks took her up and down hills with only a few level stretches. Often she would stop to pick up litter—a beer can here, a plastic cup there. Some folks trashed their beautiful surroundings without giving it a second thought.

Today she kept a steady pace, enjoying the view. A scent of pine filled the air, and a brisk breeze ruffled her hair. Up ahead, a glimmer of white caught her eye. She moved closer to the ditch. Looked like a plastic sack—a kitchen garbage bag. More trash.

Marian reached down—then stopped. This wasn't garbage. Something inside the bag moved. Her pulse quickened. Had someone discarded a kitten or a puppy from an unwanted litter? She held her breath, listening for any sounds. The bag was open. Was it a snake or some other animal foraging for scraps? Better leave it alone. She stared at the sack. Then she heard it—a faint whimper.

That sounded like a baby! Marian leaned over, reached into the ditch, and pulled back the edge of the bag. There was the little face—eyes squinched, mouth open. It *was* a baby!

A thin receiving blanket swaddled the infant inside the bag. Tiny arms and legs pushed against the cover. Carefully, she pulled out the little bundle and stood, cradling the baby in her arms.

Wonder how old it is? No more than a few hours. Her mind raced. *I need to get this baby home—call the police—get an ambulance. Oh, my God. A baby!*

Marian unzipped her jacket, placed the child next to her body, and zipped up again. She walked fast, her arms bracing the infant. The twenty minutes back to the house seemed like forever.

Pushing open the front door, Marian screamed, "Jim! Where are you?"

"Goodness, honey. What's the matter?" Her husband emerged from the kitchen.

"I found a *baby*!" She pulled the infant from under her jacket and held it up for Jim to see. "It was right by the side of the road—in the ditch." The child's lusty cries filled the room.

"A baby? Good grief. In the ditch?" Jim rushed forward and took the bundle from Marian's hands. "Shh, shh, there, little one." He gently jostled the infant.

Marian smiled. It hadn't been that many years since Jim held a newborn. Well—a few years now—their grandson, James, was sixteen.

"I bet you're hungry. Wonder where your mama is?" Jim looked up at Marian. "Better call nine-one-one."

The next hour was a flurry of activity. Police officers and paramedics arrived about the same time. They unwrapped and carefully examined the infant. Marian had been correct; the baby boy was no more than four or five hours old. The umbilical cord had been crudely tied and cut, but the infant appeared healthy, except for slight dehydration. The paramedics rewrapped the newborn in a clean receiving blanket, placed a knit cap on his head, and carried him to the ambulance. Soon everyone was gone.

Marian sank into a chair at the kitchen table. It was hard to think about eating breakfast. Jim reached for the coffee pot and poured two cups.

"I can't imagine what that mother was thinking to leave her child in a ditch like that." Marian shook her head. "What if I hadn't come along when I did? That baby could be dead by now. How could a mother do that?" Tears brimmed in her eyes.

"She had to be mighty scared," Jim said. "Even if she didn't want her baby, she could have left him at a hospital or a police station. I'm pretty sure Arkansas has a law that allows a mother to give up her baby without being identified."

"Well, I hope she comes forward," Marian said. "If she's a teenager, she may be suffering aftereffects with no one to care for her. That's terrible."

◆ ◆ ◆

Jim pushed back in his recliner and clicked on the five o'clock news. Channel 4 aired the full story. In Hot Springs Village a healthy newborn, infant boy had been found in a ditch by an early morning walker. So far, the police had no clues to the mother's identity. The baby was safe, but authorities were concerned about the mother's health. The Garland County sheriff explained how the Safe Haven Law allowed a mother, under certain conditions, to give up her child. They urged her to seek medical attention. Within a few days the baby would be turned over to the Department of Human Services.

The phone rang, and Jim pushed the mute button on the remote. "Hello?"

"Hi, Granddad."

His grandson's voice on the other end brightened his spirits. "Hi, James. How're you doing?"

"Pretty good, I guess. Mom said y'all had some excitement today." James sounded a little down.

"Sure did. You never know what you'll find when you're out walking the roads these days." Jim tried to sound light-hearted. "Your Nana was quite a heroine."

"That's for sure. Can she pick up the other phone? I need to talk with both of you."

"Marian, it's James. Can you catch the phone there in the kitchen?" He heard Marian click on.

"Hi, James. I'm here."

"Nana, I need to let you know something." James hesitated and then continued. "You know that baby you found this morning?" Another pause. "I don't know how to tell you this, but I know whose it is."

"You do?" The words burst out from both of them.

"Yes." James paused again. "It's mine."

Seconds passed in heavy silence.

Then Marian spoke. "Oh, no, James. That little boy is *yours*?"

"Yes, Marcy and I delivered him early this morning. No one knew she was pregnant. Not even her mom. She was scared to tell her."

"Marcy was pregnant?"

"Yeah. Finally, this afternoon she decided she'd better tell her mother 'cause she was bleeding so bad. I told Mom and Dad too, and we've been down talking with the police. Marcy and her mom are at the hospital."

Jim and Marian sat in stunned silence.

Then Jim spoke. "James, that is the saddest thing I've ever heard. But, tell me. Why on earth did you leave that baby out there in a ditch? What were you thinking? Some animal could have killed him, or he could have died from starvation."

"Well, they tell us now we could have left him at the hospital, but we didn't know that. Besides, Marcy still didn't want anyone to know. We thought about how Nana takes her walk every morning, so I left him where Nana would find him."

"Oh, my goodness." Marian's eyes filled with tears. "What if I hadn't come along?"

"I was right there, Nana. You couldn't see me, but I saw you pick him up."

"You did? Oh, James. What are you and Marcy going to do now?"

"I haven't talked with her since this afternoon, but I think we'll probably give the baby away. Getting pregnant was a big mistake, but trying to keep a baby now would be an even bigger mistake, I think." Their grandson tried to sound grown-up, but his voice cracked with emotion.

"Tell you what, son. Why don't you give us a few minutes to digest all this." Jim struggled to keep his voice calmer now. "We'll talk with you and your folks again in a little while. You've been real brave to tell us all this yourself. We love you."

Jim and Marian clicked off their phones.

"Oh, Jim. How could he do that? That baby is our first great-grandchild."

"I know." Jim took a deep breath. "Poor kids. Trying to have a baby without anyone knowing. Then leaving their son out in the woods. Unbelievable."

Tears welled. Jim could not control them any longer.

Author's Note: LOST AND FOUND

In June 2004 I attended my first Arkansas Writers' Conference in Little Rock. Noted fiction author Bruce Holland Rogers was our featured speaker.

Following the conference, Bruce stayed over to conduct a workshop on Sunday morning for aspiring short story writers. We paid extra for the workshop and were invited to submit a manuscript to be critiqued. The first five would be distributed ahead of time to all participants. My story "Lost and Found" was one of the five.

Being a novice writer, I had much to learn. Most experienced writers in the workshop were kind in their critiques, but I was still embarrassed. Later, after making a few changes, I submitted it to a White County Creative Writers' contest, and in September the story won second honorable mention. That boosted my confidence a little.

Thanks to my fellow writers, I now understand much more about the craft of writing. Recently, I corrected major technical flaws in the story, and I have included this revised version as an example of my persistence.

How did I get the idea for this tale? Wherever we have lived, I have picked up litter on roadsides near our homes. A mundane task, to be sure. But I've also often wondered if I would ever come across something unusual. What bizarre thing out there might be "lost and found"? This story was my answer to that question.

The Letter Writer

"What? You don't mean it!"

Mama glanced at me playing jacks there on the linoleum and then turned her back and spoke lower into the receiver. "You mean she shot her right there in the church parking lot?"

I tossed up the ball, picked up some two-sies, dropped them into my other hand, and caught the ball on the rebound.

"Well, I wonder what brought that on? Good gracious! A person's not even safe going to church anymore."

I looked up at Mama and frowned. Then I picked up some more two-sies and caught the ball again.

"Of course I will. That's the least we can do. Just tell me what I need to bring."

A pause.

"Okay. Sure. Chicken will be fine. I'll get it over to their house as soon as I can. How long will she be in the hospital?"

Another pause.

"Well, thank goodness. It's a miracle the bullet missed her heart."

Mama turned and watched me sweep up more two-sies.

"Yes, I will. Thanks for calling. Talk with you again later." She hung up the receiver.

"Who was that, Mama?"

"Just Miss Callie. Miss Marjorie is in the hospital. I'll need to help fix Mr. Tom and the boys some supper."

"Who shot her?"

Mama gave me a stern look. "You weren't supposed to hear all that."

Then she sighed. "But you might as well know, I guess. It'll be all over town. Miss Lois came riding up just as the ladies were leaving their afternoon prayer meeting, and she shot Miss Marjorie as she was coming down the steps."

"Why did she do that?"

"Nobody knows for sure. I'm just thankful she didn't kill her. They have Miss Lois down at the police station. I'm sure we'll all know why she did it soon enough. Now you need to pick up your jacks and get your shoes on. We need to run over to the grocery store."

Mama hurried out of the room, and I made one last swipe before jumping up to follow.

The next day at school everyone was talking about it. Larry and J. T. were absent. They had gone to stay with their Aunt Janie for a few days. I wondered if they had a chance to eat any of Mama's fried chicken before they left.

Susan reported what she overheard at her house. "Mother was talking with Miss Callie, and she said there was blood all over the steps. Yuck. Pastor McElroy was out there washing it off as soon as the police left."

"My mama said we're not even safe at church anymore," I said.

"Well, maybe no one else is going to shoot anybody." Betty sounded like she wasn't too sure. "Miss Callie told my mother Miss Lois shot Miss Marjorie because she wrote that Letter to the Editor."

"What letter?"

"Oh, you know. The one about how it was wrong to put all the Japs in California in those camps." Betty scowled as she spoke. "Miss Lois had a son who was killed over there at Pearl Harbor. I'm sure she was furious when Miss Marjorie said she felt sorry for those dirty Japs."

"Well, the people in those camps are all Americans, aren't they?" I could feel my face getting hot. Usually, I wasn't brave enough to speak up in our group. "I don't think *they* bombed anybody."

"Just the same, we can't be sure, can we?" Susan sounded like a real know-it-all. "My daddy says we have to protect our country. Besides, if you were Miss Lois, you sure wouldn't want someone saying things like Miss Marjorie said."

The trial lasted most of the summer. It took a while to find enough people to sit on the jury. Most folks admitted they couldn't be impartial. They finally seated twelve jurors from neighboring counties. Then the defense insisted Miss Lois should be found innocent of attempted murder because it was a crime of passion. They brought in all kinds of character witnesses.

Finally, after three full days of deliberation, the jury convicted Miss Lois of assault with a deadly weapon. She was sentenced to seven years. Later, she was released after serving only three. Many people still believed Miss Lois was justified in taking aim at Miss Marjorie. Personally, I thought Miss Marjorie was a brave champion for justice.

All of that took place over sixty years ago, and today it's as clear in my mind as if it happened only yesterday. This morning I saw another Letter to the Editor. This time the writer denounced the detainment of Arab Americans in our airports—said it was "a violation of their civil rights."

I looked to see whose name was at the bottom. James Thomas Jackson. Little J. T. I smiled. Miss Marjorie would be proud.

Author's note: THE LETTER WRITER

Immediately following September 11, 2001, the United States went on high alert. Reeling from the suicide plane attacks on the World Trade Center in New York City, the plane attack on the Pentagon in Washington, D.C., and the crash of hijacked United Airlines Flight 93 into a field near Shanksville, Pennsylvania, our government took stringent measures to deter any future terrorist activity against our citizens. Anyone resembling an Arab was detained in our airports until his identity and purpose could be determined.

However, this was not the first time our country reacted out of fear. I created this story to help us recall a similar period following December 7, 1941. Could we learn from our mistakes?

On March 28, 2005, "The Letter Writer" won third place in a Village Writers' Club short story contest.

A Broken House

Gripping the wheel, Al maneuvered the family's four-wheel drive around splintered planks and broken branches. At last, he turned into the driveway, shut off the engine, and stared, speechless, at the scene in front of him. Two huge oaks lay sprawled across the roof. He glanced at his wife. Mary's eyes met his, and he shared his pain with her in silence.

"Daddy, look. There's my bike." Katie pointed to the neighbor's chain-link fence. Her two-wheeler with training wheels dangled from the top by its handlebars.

Al managed a feeble smile. "Looks like the wind hung it right up there for you."

Mary frowned. "Honey, I don't think we should let the kids out in all this mess. Nails and broken glass are everywhere."

"Well, we need to check things inside." Al turned toward the back seat. "Kids, your mom and I won't be gone but just a minute. Y'all stay here now, okay? Then we'll come back and get you."

"But I want to see my room," Jonathan whined.

"Me, too," Katie said.

Al was in no mood to argue. "How about it, Mama?" He searched his wife's face for approval. "I can carry Katie till we get inside. Jonathan can watch where he steps."

Mary shrugged. "Okay, I know we all want to see what's happened. But, please, be careful. We don't need to deal with anything else right now."

Katie rode on Al's shoulders, and Jonathan clutched his mother's hand as the four made their way across the littered yard. Mary unlocked the door, and they entered the house.

"Oh, my God!" Her eyes brimmed with tears.

Rain-soaked debris from the attic covered the floors and furniture. Pieces of insulation drooped from soggy ceilings, and jagged rafters protruded through gaping holes. A musty odor permeated the air.

"It's bad, all right." Al set Katie down. "Let's check the rest of the house. You kids stay close to us now." He stepped through clutter into the kitchen with Jonathan right behind. "It's not quite as bad in here. The trees didn't break through in this part."

Holding Katie's hand, Mary appeared in the doorway. "You're right. This looks a little better. With the power off, we'll need to get all the food out of the refrigerator, though." She opened the door.

Al peered over her shoulder at a half bottle of milk, a carton of juice, and leftovers in plastic containers. In the crisper drawer, lettuce looked wilted. In the freezer, thawed packages of meat dripped dark brown juices, pooling on the bottom. The stench billowed out into the room.

"Whew! That's awful!" Mary slammed the compartment door and turned away.

Al, Mary, and the children moved through the house, assessing the damage. Tree branches penetrated the ceiling in both children's rooms.

"My bed's all wet," Jonathan said, patting his spread.

Katie's room was soaked too. She grabbed Bitty Baby from her doll cradle, brushed off crumbled insulation, and hugged her close. "It's okay, Baby," she crooned.

In the master bedroom, hurricane winds had ripped plywood from the window. Shards of glass lay scattered across the carpet.

Al glanced at his watch. "I guess we'd better gather what we can. Mary, you can start packing more clothes. We'll need to round up all our important papers too—our insurance information, address book—things like that. There should be empty boxes in the storeroom. I may be able to salvage food from the pantry."

Last year's family portrait hung askew above the dresser.

"I'll get our pictures and albums too," Mary said. "I hope they're not all water-logged. Kids, you need to pick out some of your games and toys. Just put them in pillow cases. We'll have to find another place to stay for a while."

Struggling to keep his emotions in check, Al reentered the kitchen. He knew his family was lucky compared with those living closer to the beach. Not a wall or tree stood for half a mile inland. But it was hard to face uncertainty. Where would they go? What about his job? What about school for Jonathan?

Thank God they evacuated. When storm warnings came, he had boarded windows and loaded his family. They landed in a motel a hundred miles north. That was five days ago. Now they were back. To enter the area, he had showed his driver's license to police to prove where he lived. Did the cop say only six hours? That wasn't much time to collect what they needed. Then the area would be closed, and they'd have to leave. No telling when they'd be able to return.

By early afternoon, the van was filled, and Al and his family headed north. He wished he'd known they'd return so soon. Now it was too late to reserve a room. His cell phone wouldn't work, and when the family arrived at their old motel, the place was full. So were many others along their route until they found a shelter in Shreveport.

That night he used a land-line phone to call his brother in Dallas. Jake's kids were in college. He and Janice would have empty bedrooms, but Al hated to impose on them. Jake had emphysema, and Janice always worried about his health.

"Hi, Bud." Al tried to sound cheerful. "We're all safe, but we may need to come visit you a few days."

"Sure. Come on." Jake coughed to one side. "We've been wondering where you were—didn't know how to get in touch with you. It's good to hear from you! When do you think you'll get here?"

"We're in a shelter in Shreveport right now. We can spend a couple nights here, if we need to. Then we'll head your way whenever it's convenient."

"No problem. Here, let me put Jan on the line." Jake coughed again.

"Hi, Al. Are all of you okay?"

"Yes, I guess we were really very lucky—just water damage inside the house where trees fell on the roof. I think our homeowner's insurance will cover everything except for the deductible. But now we need to find a place to stay for a while. If we can visit with you a few days, then we can look for an apartment."

"Of course. You know you're always welcome." Jan hesitated. "Let's see. What is today? Thursday? Why don't you and Mary and the kids plan to get here on Saturday? Then I'll have your rooms ready and plenty of groceries on hand."

Al imagined she wasn't thrilled about having four extra people in the house.

"That sounds good. Don't worry about groceries. We'll help you with those. Sorry we have to barge in on you like this."

"Oh, that's fine. We're just so thankful you're safe. Y'all be careful now, and we'll look for you about noon on Saturday. Give our love to Mary and the kids. Bye, now."

Al replaced the receiver and made his way across the crowded floor to his family. Beggars couldn't be choosers.

Katie looked up. "Daddy, how long will our house be broke?"

"I don't know, sweetheart. But we'll be staying with Uncle Jake and Aunt Janice for a little while. We'll go see them on Saturday."

Mary gave him a look. "Saturday?"

"Yep, Saturday." Al wrapped his arms around her. "Let's just take it one day at a time, okay?"

Curled on his side, Jonathan slept. Katie snuggled with Bitty Baby. Mary pulled blankets over the children and gave them each a kiss.

"It's been a long day." She yawned, stretched, and sank onto her cot.

Al moved his bed closer to hers, settled back on his pillow, and reached for her hand. "We're going to make it through this, you know."

Mary smiled. "I know. We've got each other and the kids. That's all that matters." She squeezed his hand. "I love you."

The overhead lights flickered, casting an eerie glow on the crowd. Other families settled down. A noisy air conditioning unit droned. Al shifted on his cot. No need for Katie to worry. No need for any of them to worry. It was only their *house* that was "broke." Their family wasn't hurt. That would be so much worse.

Al savored that thought, letting it tumble over and over in his mind. Just a broken *house*—not a broken *home*—just a broken *house*. The tension slipped away. He closed his eyes. Finally, he slept.

Author's note: A BROKEN HOUSE

On Sunday evening, August 28, 2005, Hurricane Katrina blasted the Mississippi Gulf Coast. Laura Riser, my dear friend since high school, and her son, Doug, and his family had permission to ride out the storm in the Stennis Space Center where Doug worked.

All night they huddled in the dark interior, listening as 175-mile-per-hour winds and torrential rain pounded the huge concrete structure. Sections of the roof were torn away, but they remained safe. When they emerged the next morning, the scene revealed nothing but devastation. Cautiously, they made their way several miles inland to Doug's mother-in-law's house which was still intact, and there they resided for a number of weeks.

Laura's apartment in Long Beach was flooded, and many of her possessions were destroyed. Eventually, she moved to Brentwood, Tennessee, to stay with her daughter Carole and her family for nearly a year before moving back to the coast.

I wrote this story to reveal the heartbreak of a young family returning to their "broken house" following one of the deadliest hurricanes in the history of the United States.

In June 2006 "A Broken House" won first honorable mention in the Robbi Rice Dietrich Award at Arkansas Writers' Conference.

Best Laid Plans

Virginia waited while Danielle emptied the cash register, completed a deposit slip, and placed the day's receipts into two zippered bags. It was almost ten. The experienced clerk knew her young manager hated to work these late weekend hours. Danielle often complained about having no social life. "If you want to go ahead, I'll lock up behind you," Virginia said.

"Thanks." Danielle gave her a grateful smile. "It's been a long day. I'll see you Monday morning."

◆ ◆ ◆

Clutching the bags under her coat, Danielle pushed open the back door and headed toward her car.

"You can stop right there."

She jumped. The gruff voice in her ear came out of nowhere.

"Just give me the money and you won't get hurt."

Something hard pressed against her side.

"Okay, okay. I'll give it to you. Please don't hurt me." She turned and threw down the bags.

The man in a ski mask scrambled to get them and took off running toward his truck just as Virginia opened the door and stepped outside.

"I've been robbed!" screamed Danielle. "There he goes."

"Oh, my God!" Virginia jumped back as the dark pickup squealed past them, spewing exhaust. "I think I saw his tag number." She fumbled in her purse, retrieved her cell, and pressed nine-one-one. "I want to report a robbery behind Clara's Boutique at Oakmont Square. A man just grabbed our deposit and fled in a black pickup. I believe his license begins with the numbers 679. I'm not sure about the letters—maybe an H was in there." She waited. "Yes, it was an Arkansas plate." Another pause. "All right, we'll stay here until they arrive."

In less than five minutes, a squad car pulled into the lot. Two officers stepped out and escorted them back into the store. Danielle gave an account of what happened, and although her descriptions of the thief and his truck were sketchy, the duplicate deposit slip showed the exact amount stolen. The policemen thanked them and left. Still shaken, she and Virginia each headed for home.

♦ ♦ ♦

Monday morning, two detectives entered the store. One of them stepped forward. "Danielle Curtis?"

"Yes?"

"Miss Curtis, you are under arrest."

"What's going on?" Virginia moved from behind the counter. "You can't just come in here and arrest the manager for no reason."

"This woman is charged with theft of more than twenty-five hundred dollars and filing a false police report." The officer clamped on the handcuffs and read Danielle her rights.

Virginia frowned. "Danielle, tell him. You don't know anything about this."

The young woman twisted around to face her accuser. "She's right. I don't know what you're talking about."

The detective smirked. "Oh, yeah? That getaway truck was registered to your old boyfriend. And how do you explain those bank bags in the dumpster behind Freyer's apartment?"

"Tim didn't do this. I swear. It had to be some other guy."

"You'll have plenty of time to give us your story downtown." The officer grabbed Danielle's arm and shoved her outside and into a patrol car.

The car pulled away from the curb, leaving Virginia speechless in the doorway.

Monday afternoon the detectives returned. Virginia told them everything she knew—things her co-worker had confided in her several weeks ago. Yes, Danielle was seeing Tim again, but she had insisted he was a changed man. He had served his time and cleaned up his act and was no longer doing drugs. Were the police really sure he took the money? What about a motive?

Danielle did say Tim was worried about some guy who hounded him about a loan he needed to pay back. But Danielle and Tim wouldn't have risked stealing funds from the shop—not with him just out of prison and on parole. As manager of the store, Danielle made a good salary, plus her commission. It would have been easy for them to save the money and pay off the debt.

That night, Virginia tossed and turned, replaying the conversation in her mind. Rolling over, she touched her husband's shoulder.

"I'm worried, Frank. You know I've never been involved in anything like this before."

"Just take it one day at a time," he said. "You did all you could. Danielle and that loser boyfriend of hers are each being held on ten thousand dollars' bail. I doubt if they'll be out of jail anytime soon. On the news tonight they said Freyer's only alibi is that he was home watching TV. That's pretty lame. You need to get some sleep." Frank pecked her on the cheek and then turned away.

Okay, she would try to relax and think pleasant thoughts—forget about her worries. Actually, the robbery had gone quite well—just as they planned. The police had their suspects, and she and Frank had the money—almost five thousand dollars in cash. It was only a matter of time until they could enjoy it. She thought about all those wealthy women who shopped in the store. Now it would be her turn to show up in the latest fashion. She might even splurge on some expensive perfume.

◆ ◆ ◆

Virginia clicked on "Print," pushed back her chair from the computer, and stood to stretch. Her story was almost finished. The next part would be harder to write—her discovery of the plane tickets—one for Frank and one for *Ruth*, that mousy little secretary of his. To think Frank would steal all that money for a trip to Hawaii with *Ruth*. God! That still made her so mad! Finally, Virginia's decision to call the police, even knowing she and Frank would both be arrested. Then the trial and verdict. Not a pretty ending.

The matron stepped over to the cubicle. "Your time is up for today."

Virginia gathered her sheets from the printer and slipped them into an envelope. Escorted by the guard, she trudged down the corridor to her cell.

Author's note: BEST LAID PLANS

This story was my first attempt at writing a mystery. Most of my fictional stories spring from personal experiences or from those I hear or read about. But this one was completely imaginary.

I did work as a clerk in a dress shop one time, but the closest I ever came to a crime was when I confronted a young shoplifter. She yanked the blouse out of her purse, threw it down, and ran.

During the 2005–2006 club year, Village Writers' Club sponsored a mystery contest. "Best Laid Plans" won second place. On September 2, 2006, the story placed third in a contest calling for "mystery or suspense short story" sponsored by White County Creative Writers.

Finally, in June 2007 at Arkansas Writers' Conference, "Best Laid Plans" was awarded second honorable mention out of forty-one entries in the Francis Rossini Memorial mystery contest.

It was fun to create this tale of intrigue and suspense.

Behind Closed Doors

One solemn eye peered out from behind the partially-opened door. A chain blocked my entry.

"Timmy, is your mommy home?" I hoped my smile would reassure the four-year-old I wasn't a threat.

"She's at work."

"Well, sweetie, I'm the lady who lives next door. Did you call me?"

"Nana's on the floor."

"If you'll let me come in, maybe I can help her get up, okay?"

The door slammed. Something scraped across the floor. Then I heard fumbling and rattling. In a moment the door opened, and Timmy pulled back a chair to let me enter.

I glanced around but saw only toys on the floor. David always left his playthings scattered too. I still missed him so much.

"Where is your nana, Timmy?"

"Back there." He pointed toward a closed door.

"Hello?" I called. No response. I crossed the room, turned the knob, and pushed open the door. Beside the bed, a heavyset woman about my age lay sprawled in a pool of blood. Her ashen face showed no sign of life. "Oh, my God."

"Nana's sick."

Timmy's eyes searched mine, and I steadied myself. "Where's your phone, sweetheart? We need to call nine-one-one."

"In the kitchen."

I hurried to a wall phone near the back door. After punching in numbers, I waited, my heart pounding in my ears.

When police and paramedics arrived, they determined Timmy's grandmother had died from a stab wound in her back, although no weapon was found. Thankfully, the child didn't see it happen. Timmy told the officers he was playing in the back yard, and when he came inside to potty, he found Nana on the floor. Seeing my number taped by the phone, he crawled up onto a chair and called me.

A female officer took over the care of Timmy and gave me permission to leave. Moments later, Timmy's mother, Monica, arrived. Her compact screeched to a halt by the curb. I watched from my window as she leaped out, bounded up the front steps, and burst into the house. Her distant wails of grief overwhelmed me, and I sank onto the couch.

Who could do such a gruesome thing? My God! A cold-blooded killer had been right next door, and I hadn't noticed a thing. No strange cars or trucks. No loud noises. Nothing.

Later, I watched a man—probably the coroner—transport the covered body on a gurney to a van. Shortly after that, Monica loaded suitcases and Timmy into her car and drove away. I didn't blame her for leaving. The police remained until dark—I supposed to collect more evidence.

The week passed slowly. I found myself pacing from room to room, fidgeting with this and that, jumping at every sound. I kept all my doors and windows locked but still didn't feel safe. After all, a killer had entered Monica's house with the front door chain-locked. How did he get in? Through the back? Why wouldn't Timmy have seen him? It all seemed too strange.

Friday morning the doorbell rang. From the front window I spotted a pot-bellied man in a short-sleeved shirt standing on my porch.

He noticed me and flashed a badge attached to his wallet.

"Lorraine Wilson?"

I nodded. His deep voice could be heard through the window.

"I'm Detective Joe Braden, here to ask a few questions."

I ushered him into the living room. "Please have a seat. Would you like a cup of coffee?"

"No, thank you, ma'am. This won't take long. I just need to check on a few things."

He slipped a small notebook from the back pocket of his wrinkled trousers, lifted a pen from his shirt pocket, clicked it, and settled into the armchair across the room.

Perched on the edge of my couch, I waited.

"Mrs. Wilson, how long have you known Monica Simmons?"

"Not long. She and Timmy moved in last month. I carried them some cookies a few days later, and we visited a while. Can't say we shared more than small talk."

"Were you aware she was divorced?"

"Yes, she mentioned her former husband lived out of state. Timmy gets to see him once or twice a year, I think."

"What about her mother—the deceased? Did you know her too?"

"No, I knew she babysat with Timmy sometimes, but she wasn't a regular visitor. Most days Timmy was in daycare." That awful sight in the bedroom flashed through my mind, and I shuddered. "Poor woman!"

The detective frowned. "Well, apparently, she was surprised. There wasn't a sign of a struggle." He paused, checking his notes. "You said the boy had to unlock the door to let you in?"

"Yes, that's what I told the officers. Did they ever discover how the killer got in?"

"They're still working on that."

His abrupt tone let me know he'd revealed enough.

"Did Monica ever talk about any trouble she was having with her former husband?"

"She mentioned him missing a few payments. Said she was making it okay, though. She told me she worked for some insurance agency."

"What about her mother. Any problems there?"

"I'm really not sure. Like I said, I don't know Monica very well. We're just neighbors, that's all."

The detective closed his notebook and slipped the pen back into his pocket. He stood and smiled. "Appreciate your help, ma'am." He handed me a business card. "If anything else comes to mind, give me a call."

I rose and shook his hand. "I'm afraid I haven't been much help. But good luck with your investigation. I'll rest a lot easier when you find whoever did this terrible thing."

After he left, I walked back to the kitchen and posted his card with a magnet to the refrigerator door.

Tuesday morning's front page headline was a shock: "Local Woman Arrested in Death of Mother." Trembling, I set my mug on the kitchen table and studied the grainy photo. Yes, that was Monica being escorted by two uniformed officers to their car.

I scanned the article. There had been no sign of forced entry so the police suspected the victim knew the perpetrator. Monica and her mother had a stormy past. The young woman's drug addiction had prompted her mother to call authorities several times to remove Timmy from the home. The police suspected she threatened to do that again. They alleged the two women argued, and, in a fit of rage, Monica stabbed her mother before leaving for work that morning. She left her son playing in the yard, knowing he would discover his grandmother.

I couldn't believe what I was reading. How could a mother leave a four-year-old alone to find his grandmother lying in a pool of blood?

Poor Timmy. He must be so confused—his grandmother gone and his mother arrested. What would become of him now?

I thought of my own little David—another innocent victim. Many a night I kept my grandson here while Cheryl and that no-account husband of hers entertained their low-life friends. After one of their binges, she and I would go round and round, but I couldn't talk any sense into her. She never admitted she had a problem. "Mom," she'd say, "just butt out, will you? Jim and I are fine. We're both working. It's not like we're a couple of drunks."

But I could see what it was doing to David. When Cheryl and Jim drank, they paid little attention to him. I knew I couldn't protect him forever, and I felt so helpless! Sometimes I thought they kept right on drinking just to spite me.

Then my worst fears came true. Coming home from a day at the lake, Jim was driving drunk. Their van missed a curve, crashed into a tree, and burst into flames. Cheryl and Jim died on the scene, and I lost my precious David two days later.

Even after all these years, just thinking about it made my blood boil. If Cheryl had listened to me, she and David would still be alive.

The following Tuesday my telephone rang.

"Hello, Mrs. Wilson. This is Monica Simmons."

"Monica? My goodness. How are you?"

"Well, they turned me loose, and I'd like to come by, if you're going to be home."

Her request caught me off guard. "Ah ... that'll be fine. I'll be here."

She thanked me, and I clicked off the phone.

Monica must be out on bail. Why would she want to see *me*? Maybe she needed money. Maybe she was back on drugs.

My stomach churned.

Ten minutes later, Monica stood at my door.

"I hope I'm not interrupting anything."

"No, this is a good time." I eyed her carefully. "Come on in."

She entered, and I turned toward the kitchen. "Let's go back here, and I'll make us some coffee."

"That would be nice. I can't stay long, though. I just stopped next door to pick up a few things, and I thought I'd step over to say hi."

While the coffee dripped, we continued our conversation at the kitchen table.

"I guess you wonder why I'm not in jail," she said. "They let me post bond because they have another suspect now."

"They do? I'm sure you're glad about that." Still wary, I managed a smile. "I haven't seen anything in the paper, though."

"You probably won't. This time they don't want to do anything to jeopardize their case."

She dropped her eyes, fiddled with a hang nail on her thumb, and then looked up.

"They've questioned a guy who stole Mama's car. She drove it to my house when she came to stay with Timmy. Last week they found it in a chop shop across the state line. It had parts missing, but they still identified it. When the sheriff busted the fellows running the shop, they told him who sold them her car."

Chop shop? Busted? Monica's vocabulary surprised me.

"Do they think he killed your mother?"

"Yeah."

"Well, it was all a terrible tragedy. I'm so sorry, Monica." I reached over and patted her hand.

"Thanks. Mama and I had our problems, but lately we'd been getting along pretty good." She reached for a tissue in her pocket.

I waited a moment. "How about that cup of coffee now?"

I rose and moved to the counter. My sleeping pills stood by the sink. Quietly, I slipped four tablets into her drink.

An hour later, I punched in the number on the detective's card.

"Joe Braden here."

"Detective, this is Lorraine Wilson." My voice broke into sobs. "Please come … right away. I … I … just killed Monica Simmons."

"What? Hold on now. Hold on. I'll be right there."

The phone went dead, and I laid it on the table. Picking up the bloody knife, I cut my arms in a few places and dropped it on the floor.

Monica's story about another suspect was all a lie, of course—a vicious lie. I knew it the moment she said her mother drove to her house. There was never another car in the driveway that night or the next morning, either. Her mother wasn't killed by an intruder who stole her car. Ridiculous! The woman on my floor was an evil drug abuser who murdered her own mother—a woman whose lies should never be believed—a woman not fit to be Timmy's mother—a woman who deserved to die!

The pills made it easy. While asleep, she couldn't resist. I'd tell the detective she was on drugs again and demanded money. When I refused, she became angry, whipped out the knife, and tried to stab me like she stabbed her mother. But I grabbed the knife and plunged it into her heart.

Drugs can do crazy things to people—drugs and alcohol. This time an innocent child would not have to suffer. My precious David was gone, but now, little Timmy was safe. He deserved a good home. He could live with me and have a new nana.

Smiling, I sat at my table and waited.

Author's note: BEHIND CLOSED DOORS

After winning an award for "Best Laid Plans" in the Francis Rossini Memorial mystery contest at Arkansas Writers' Conference in 2007, I noticed a similar contest, the Al Rossini Memorial Award, listed in the AWC brochure for 2008. I decided to try my hand at another mystery. But this time, I needed a lot more input from my critique group.

The surprise ending in "Behind Closed Doors" had to be believable, so the killer's mindset needed to be established early in the story. However, clues could not be too obvious. My writer friends and I had fun brainstorming ideas.

"Behind Closed Doors" won first honorable mention out of twenty-eight entries in the Rossini mystery contest that year. On August 30, 2008, the story was awarded another first honorable mention at White County Creative Writers' Conference.

Death Comes Walking

No one seemed too surprised when they found the old man's body on Cedar Creek Trail. After all, residents die every week in this retirement community. Nevertheless, I still worried about his wife. What a distressing experience, to have your pet show up at home, dragging his leash, with your husband nowhere in sight.

Then yesterday, his wife's body was found—on that same walking trail. Strange. My friend Mildred called me. She knew the couple—the Hoffstetlers lived right across the street—so she was pretty upset. Not many spouses die outdoors in the same location within a month of each other.

Vernon and Gertrude Hoffstetler were in their eighties, she said, and both suffered with diabetes and mild dementia, but they seemed to manage okay with a caregiver coming in three days a week. They had no children, only a few nieces and nephews in California. No family members came to Vernon's memorial service—just the caregiver and a few neighbors.

This morning Mildred called me again—said she hadn't slept a wink. I went over to her house, and we sat at the kitchen table, drank coffee, and talked.

"I know you'll miss your friends," I said, patting her hand. "I'm so sorry for your loss."

"Thank you, dear. I'm already missing them terribly. But Edith, that's not all. I'm just not convinced Gertrude's death was from natural causes." She stared at her cup and stirred her already-stirred coffee. "There was no sign of foul play, but it seems so bizarre."

"The police talked with all the neighbors, right?"

"Two officers came around yesterday afternoon. They picked up Buddy too and took him to the animal shelter." Mildred removed the spoon from her cup and took a sip. She looked up, her bleary eyes blinking fast.

"What about the couple's caregiver? Seems like she'd be able to provide the most information."

Mildred shrugged. "I don't know. She wasn't at the house yesterday. The police probably contacted her, but she lives down in Hot Springs. Her name's Josie Ledbetter, and she's only worked for the Hoffstetlers since January. Good worker, though, I guess. Real dependable. Gertrude liked her."

"You don't suspect she had anything to do with your neighbor's death, do you?" I was grasping at straws.

"I don't know. Like I said, she wasn't even there."

Mildred took another sip. Her hands shook as she lowered the cup, and I reached across the table to pat her on the arm. "Well, maybe something will turn up. In the meantime, don't go for a walk on Cedar Creek Trail."

Mildred gave me a weak smile. "No chance of that."

I watched for another article in our weekly newspaper, and sure enough, one appeared the following Wednesday. The headline spread over three columns: "Second Death Occurs on Village Trail."

A color photo showed delicate wildflowers at the base of the Cedar Creek sign with leafy green branches overhead. The reporter covered the unusual occurrence of Gertrude's death but was careful not to add anything to cause further alarm. According to police reports, both Mr. and Mrs. Hoffstetler appeared to have died from natural causes, but autopsies were underway.

After that, things settled down for a few days. Mildred and I visited again, and she seemed to enjoy telling me more about the Hoffstetlers. During their early years in Hot Springs Village, Mildred and her husband, Jacob, played bridge every week with Vernon and Gertrude, and the two couples developed a warm friendship. However, Jacob was gone now too, and I understood why her neighbors' sudden deaths caused Mildred such pain. I vowed to visit more often.

One week later, Mildred called, almost hysterical. Early morning joggers discovered *another* body on Cedar Creek Trail. The deceased, Velma Brinkstone, was a close friend of the Hoffstetlers.

"Goodness, Mildred. This is terrible!"

"It's just so sad," Mildred cried. "Velma was the dearest little lady you could ever know. She and Gertrude looked out for each other. Velma wasn't quite as sharp as she used to be, and Gertrude introduced her to Darlene, Josie's daughter, so Velma could have a caregiver too."

"Well, I'm sure you must be devastated," I said. "This is unbelievable."

"Velma liked to walk the trail with Vernon and Gertrude, but I can't believe she died right there in the same place."

"Something sinister is definitely going on," I said. "The police will step up now, I'm sure."

I was right. Officers closed Cedar Creek Trail and patrolled the area day and night. Officials urged nearby residents to report any suspicious activity. The Village buzzed with concern. Everywhere we went, people talked about the "walking trail deaths"—at church, at Walmart, on the golf courses, at the post office. Meanwhile, autopsies on the three bodies continued. I hoped we'd learn something soon.

Finally, a front page article in the *Hot Springs Village Voice* seemed to confirm our suspicions. Medical findings revealed Vernon Hoffstetler died from coronary thrombosis—a massive heart attack. However, Gertrude Hoffstetler had traces of lethal drugs in her system, and Velma Brinkstone died from the same cause. Police continued their investigation.

Mildred and I met for supper to discuss the latest developments.

"I suppose their deaths could be suicides," I said.

Mildred shook her head. "Gertrude grieved for Vernon, but I doubt if she was depressed enough to kill herself. And Velma seemed okay too."

"Do you think they were murdered?"

My friend glanced away and then took a deep breath. "I'm afraid so. And I'll tell you who did it." Her eyes met mine. "Josie and Darlene."

"The caregivers?"

"Right. It had to be them. They both had access to their employers' medicines."

"That's true, but why would they do it?" I frowned. "I thought you said Gertrude was kind to Josie, even got her daughter that job taking care of Velma."

"She was kind, all right, but almost too kind, if you know what I mean. Gertrude loaned money to Josie all the time, and I think Josie took advantage of her. Gertrude was forgetful, so I worried about her."

"That could be a problem. Didn't you tell me your Jacob gave away most of your savings when he had Alzheimer's?"

Mildred nodded. "Yes, that happened about a year before he died. He was swindled out of thousands of dollars by his nephew, Dan. I didn't even find out until after Jacob's death." She paused, struggling to regain composure. "Dan never repaid a dime."

"Well, I guess the police will investigate Josie's and Darlene's involvement with the Hoffstetlers and Mrs. Brinkstone," I said. "I'm sure they'll get to the bottom of it."

On my way home, I replayed our conversation. Mildred seemed so sure the caregivers were guilty. But if Josie was getting extra money from Mrs. Hoffstetler, why would she kill her? That didn't make sense. And what about Velma Brinkstone? Why kill her too? Unless ... unless somehow the caregivers could get even *more* money with both of their employers dead. Yes, that was bound to be it. Greed was a powerful motive.

Gertrude and Velma might have decided to include their faithful employees in their wills. After all, neither widow seemed to have many relatives. If Josie and Darlene knew they were about to inherit thousands of dollars, or maybe even more, that would certainly be an incentive to speed things up—give their employers an overdose and stage it to look like they died on the trail.

I tapped the steering wheel and smiled. I couldn't wait to call Mildred.

Neither of us was surprised when Hot Springs officers arrested Josie and Darlene Ledbetter on suspicion of murder. Police confirmed the women were beneficiaries in the wills.

The following week I got the biggest shock of my life.

Both caregivers were *released* because Mildred confessed *she* was the one who prepared the lethal cocktails for Gertrude and Velma!

Mildred loved her friends. What on earth happened?

I visited her in jail before the sentencing, and we sat at counters on opposite sides of a Plexiglas partition in the visitors' room.

"Edith, I'm so ashamed for you to see me in here." Mildred spoke into a phone but dropped her eyes. Her disheveled hair and drawn face made her appear older. I glanced at other inmates and visitors around us.

Holding the receiver away from my ear and lips, I responded. "Well, I don't mind telling you, this has really thrown me for a loop. We all thought for sure those Ledbetter women were guilty."

"I know. It would have been so easy to turn my back and let them go to trial. But my conscience wouldn't let me do it." She sighed and looked up, her eyes searching my face.

I stared at my friend and shook my head. "That's why I still can't get over this, Mildred. You're the kindest person I know."

Tears sprang to her eyes. "Edith, I just couldn't let those dear old ladies suffer the way my Jacob did," she said. "Their minds were getting worse and worse. All I wanted was to help them slip away in peace. It wasn't hard to do. I kept some sleeping pills from Jacob's last days."

"Oh, Mildred. How sad."

"After Vernon died, Gertrude was all alone and so vulnerable. Cedar Creek was such a beautiful place. I knew she'd want to die close to where her husband died, so we went for a walk. Afterwards, we sat on a bench by the trail, and she drank the water with the dissolved pills."

My mind struggled to grasp the picture—two friends seated side by side, one slowly dying.

"And I guess you thought Velma needed saving too?"

Mildred nodded. "Josie's daughter, Darlene, was just like her mother. She kept asking for money. Soon Velma would have given her everything."

"So you took her out to die in the same place as Gertrude?"

"I couldn't bear to leave Velma behind all alone."

A uniformed officer moved in our direction.

"I'll be back," I promised. My voice sounded steadier than I felt. We hung up our phones, and I gave her a smile. Fighting back tears, I watched the guard usher her from the room.

Author's note: DEATH COMES WALKING

My husband and I live in Hot Springs Village, Arkansas, which is located in the Ouachita Mountains about ten miles north of Hot Springs. This gated community covers approximately twenty-six thousand acres with eight golf courses, seven lakes, numerous walking trails, and about fourteen thousand residents—a peaceful place with very little crime. It would be highly unusual to have a murder take place right here in the Village. I gave my imagination free rein to come up with this one!

In September 2009 "Death Comes Walking" won third place for Mystery in a contest sponsored by the Pen Point Group at White County Creative Writers' Conference.

The Other Side of the Bed

Marge pulled up to the front of the rehab center. "Okay, dear. Wait here now. I'll get the walker for you."

She stepped from the car, hurried around to the other side, and opened the back door. Gusting winds tugged at her clothes and ruffled her hair as she struggled to hoist the metal device from the back seat to the pavement. She spread the sides and clicked them into place. Rain hadn't started yet, but dark clouds threatened to turn loose any moment. She opened the passenger door and set the walker in front of her husband.

Bill grasped the handles and stood, balancing on his left leg, his right leg suspended. "Thanks. I believe I can make it all right." He hobbled through the automatic doors into the building with Marge trailing behind.

This was her first visit to the center. Bill had been coming here three times a week since arthroscopic surgery on his left shoulder the month before, but he'd been able to drive himself with his right hand. His knee surgery the previous Friday put an end to that. Now Marge would be the chauffeur until Bill completed all rehab on his shoulder and his knee.

The open lobby was cheerful and brightly lit. Weight machines dotted the room, and busy treadmills lined the wall. CNN newscasters chatted about late-breaking events from a television attached high overhead. Bill made his way to the check-in counter and signed his name on the roster. Then he and Marge took a seat in the waiting area.

She glanced at his face, jaw set, brow furrowed. She knew his leg bothered him, but he refused to take pain meds before the appointment. "I need to tell the therapist when my shoulder hurts," he told her. His range of motion improved with each session, but now the new surgery on his knee complicated things. To use the walker, he had to put more pressure on his shoulder.

An assistant appeared with a heavy heating pad. "Here you go, Bill. Carole will be with you in a moment." She placed the pad on his shoulder.

They waited. Marge slipped the newspaper's daily crossword out of her purse, glad she remembered to bring something to pass the time. Carole appeared, greeted Bill, and smiled at Marge as she shook her hand.

Bill and the attractive forty-something moved to a treatment room. Marge sighed and gave her wind-blown hair a quick fluff and pat. Next week she'd need to get color again, if she could ever work in a time. It would be hard to get away.

She looked at her puzzle. What was a "tango need"? Three letters?

The weekend had been tough. Bill's pain seemed relentless. Surprisingly, the knee wasn't a problem, but his calf swelled and ached. Every two hours she placed fresh ice packs around it as he reclined in his easy chair with his foot elevated on a pillow.

She missed Bill's assistance around the house, especially in the mornings—retrieving the paper while she checked her e-mail, fixing the coffee, unloading the dishwasher from the night before. They'd been retired over ten years and shared most household tasks. She still handled the laundry chores, but Bill loaded the dishwasher after every meal. He even had his own way of arranging the dishes. With all her club and church activities and his golf dates three or four times a week, they were a busy and happy couple. Until now.

After Bill's shoulder surgery, Marge gave herself a pep talk. "I can do this. I'm organized. We can get through this without much hassle." And they did. Hardly missed a beat. But Bill's unexpected knee surgery put a new wrinkle in their routine. This time he needed much more attention and care.

The next day his pain grew worse. At breakfast he took more medication and dozed most of the morning. As she passed through the room, she noticed his drooping head, his gaping mouth and ashen face, and it startled her.

He looks terrible. And so old! She gently stroked his forehead, but he didn't move. "Bill, wake up, dear. It's almost lunchtime." His eyelids fluttered, and he opened milky eyes, gazing at her with a vacant stare. She smiled. "You were really out of it."

He cleared his throat and shook his head. "I can't stay awake."

"Well, I'm heating some soup. Would you like a sandwich too?"

"Okay. What time is it?"

"About twelve thirty. How're you feeling?"

"Not too bad. But I'm still in La-La Land." He struggled to stand with his walker and then hobbled to the kitchen table.

That night after supper she helped him make his way into the bedroom, get undressed, and crawl under the covers. After her bath, she walked around to the left side of the bed and quietly pulled back the sheets. It still seemed strange to sleep on that side. For almost fifty years she'd slept on the right, even in hotels. Now Bill needed to be closer to the bathroom. It was only a few steps away, and he wouldn't have to maneuver his walker so far.

Marge lay there listening to his heavy breathing. Her man was having a hard time. He turned seventy-five on his last birthday, and soon she'd be seventy. Neither of them could bounce back like they used to. The years were passing fast. Blinking back tears, she rolled onto her side and closed her eyes.

On Wednesday Bill called his doctor. "I'm still having severe pain in my right calf." Leaning over the kitchen counter, he listened intently. "Okay. We'll be there."

Marge waited.

"That was the nurse. She said Dr. Becker would call us, but they'll go ahead and schedule an ultrasound, just to make sure nothing serious is going on," he said.

About an hour later, the doctor called, and Marge and Bill headed to the hospital for the two o'clock test. In the waiting area, she scanned a magazine and tried not to worry. An hour later, the technician emerged with her husband in a wheelchair.

"Good news." She smiled. "There are no clots in any of the deep veins, just some minor obstruction in surface vessels. We'll call Dr. Becker and send him the report. He'll call you."

They thanked her, and Marge wheeled her husband down the hall and awkwardly backed the chair into the elevator. Down in the front lobby, a volunteer took over as she left to get the car and bring it around to the entrance. On the way home, she and Bill didn't say much. He grimaced every time she turned a corner or hit a small bump.

The rest of the week was busy. Bill continued to take his medication, and Marge kept his leg packed in ice. She sent numerous e-mails to her committee members, trying to stay on top of things. But she still needed to attend an important meeting. A bit uneasy about what to do, she decided to leave Bill by himself. Later, she also made a quick run to the grocery store, glad to be free but feeling guilty too.

On Friday they were back at the physical therapy center. Carole greeted them again, and Bill hobbled off for his shoulder treatment.

Marge noticed a familiar figure on one of the weight machines, and she waved. The woman smiled. Then Marge remembered who she was—Ruth Maxwell, a member of her church.

Ruth finished her exercise, walked over, and sat beside Marge. "Hi, there. I haven't seen you here before."

"Bill's here for therapy on his shoulder," Marge said. "But he just had knee surgery too, so I'm doing all the driving."

"I know how that goes. Dick's been coming here for several months."

Marge recalled something she heard at church. "Didn't he have a stroke?"

"No, they think he may have had a small seizure, but his main problem is dementia. About ten years ago he had a shunt inserted in his brain to relieve some pressure. After that he did well for a while, but lately he's been going downhill. I'm going to take him back up to Mayo in a few weeks."

Ruth looked away, and Marge followed her gaze. An elderly man walked the indoor track with two therapists. He shuffled along with a cane. "Pick up your feet, Dick," they coached. "Lift those feet. Don't drag them."

Ruth sighed. "The seizure affected his right side. It's hard for him to use that cane in his left hand. He's trying, but he just can't remember what to do very long at a time."

Marge nodded. "I'm sure you must be worried about him."

Ruth smiled. "Yes. I haven't been able to come to many of the women's meetings at church this year or my club meetings, either. Taking care of Dick is a full-time job. But I'm eager to get him back to where he was before he had the shunt put in."

Ruth looked tired. This caregiver role was no fun, but some had it much harder than others.

The next morning Marge rose early, showered, and dressed. Bill was asleep, and the room was dark. As she started into the kitchen, she slammed into the bedroom door.

"Oh, my God!"

The door's sharp edge caught her on the right brow bone, and pain surged through her head. She struggled to the chair beside the bed and fought back tears.

Startled, Bill jumped up and limped to her side. "What happened? Are you okay?" He leaned over her.

"I just walked into the damn door," she cried. "It was partly open, and I didn't see it."

"Oh, honey. I'm so sorry."

Man, this was ridiculous. Here they were—his leg hurting and her head throbbing—each trying to console one another. She laughed through her tears and reached up to hug his neck. "I don't think the skin is broken. I don't feel any blood. I'll put some ice on it. You be careful now."

Marge helped him to the bathroom and then retrieved one of his ice packs from the kitchen freezer. She placed it over her eye.

What a crazy time of life. She thought about Ruth and Dick. People had to carry on, but she and Bill were fortunate. He would get well.

Author's note: THE OTHER SIDE OF THE BED

During the spring of 2008, my husband, Robin, underwent shoulder surgery and knee surgery within four weeks of each other. Unfortunately, the arthroscopic repair on his knee was unsuccessful, so in early June he had one more surgery on his knee—a full knee replacement. His recovery that summer was long, tedious, and slow.

This was a new experience for both of us. He had to accept his limitations and be patient, and I had to accept my new role as a full-time caregiver. We had no idea how exhausting and emotionally draining these tasks could be. As a result, we both developed much empathy and respect for others in similar situations.

"The Other Side of the Bed" is a true account of our experiences following the first two surgeries. However, I patterned the characters Bill and Marge after my husband and me, changed the names of other people as well, and wrote the story as fiction.

On November 8, 2008, "The Other Side of the Bed" won first honorable mention for Fiction Short Story at the Maumelle Writers' Conference.

Encounter

~

Caught in a five-mile string of semis, SUVs, vans, and automobiles, Clyde and Martha inched past noisy road repair crews. At last, they reached the head of the line, broke loose to freedom, and were on their way again. By the time they reached their favorite Cracker Barrel twenty miles east of Memphis, the parking lot had several empty spaces.

Clyde glanced at the clock. "One fifteen. No wonder my stomach's growling." He turned off the ignition and pulled out the key.

"At least we shouldn't have to wait." Martha gathered her purse, and the two stepped out of the car.

A middle-aged woman, nicely dressed, waved and moved in their direction from the next parking aisle. "Are you folks from Arkansas?" She must have spotted their tag.

"Yes," Clyde said.

"Are you from Little Rock? Or from somewhere close to there?"

"We're from Hot Springs Village, just south of Little Rock," Martha said. The woman held an open road map. Maybe she needed directions.

"Well, you probably know that truck stop this side of Little Rock—that Petro station where I-440 comes into I-40? I stopped there this morning, and somebody broke into my car and stole my purse. Took every bit of my cash and all my credit cards."

Her eyes darted from face to face.

"That's terrible," Martha said. "Don't you have someone you can call?"

"No, my husband died last month, and I'm on my way to Bristol, Virginia. Do you think you folks could help me a little? I'm really sorry to

Views from an Empty Nest

ask for money like this, but I just don't know what else to do. I'm about out of gas." Tears brimmed in her eyes.

Martha hesitated and glanced at Clyde.

The woman continued. "I'll be glad to give you these or my rings as payment." She touched the diamond studs in her ears and then stuck out her hand with two sparkly bands on her fingers.

"Oh, you don't need to do that," Martha said. "I'm sure we can give you a little something." She turned toward her husband. "We can spare at least a twenty, don't you think?"

Clyde slipped a worn wallet out of his pocket, opened the bill compartment, and handed the woman the money.

"That's not enough for a tank of gas, but maybe it will help," Martha said with a smile.

"Oh, yes, dear. Thank you so much. I hope you folks can see I'm not just trying to get away with something here. If you will give me your address, I'll be glad to return your money."

Clyde frowned. "No, that's okay. Good luck to you now."

"Thanks, I need all the luck I can get. Would you believe I also hit a deer outside Texarkana this morning?" She motioned toward her windshield. "This has been some trip."

Martha could see a crack zig-zagged from bottom to top. "You poor thing." She reached for her hand.

"Well, maybe I can make it from here without any more trouble." The woman smiled and clasped Martha's hand. "I was married to a policeman, so you think I'd know better than to leave my purse in the car like that, even with it locked. I'll give you some advice. Don't ever travel with all your cash and credit cards in your purse, okay? Put some in your glove compartment."

"I will," Martha said. "What about lunch? Have you had anything to eat?"

"Oh, honey. I'm not hungry. After all that's happened, I don't have any appetite. They gave me some crackers back at the truck stop, so I'm fine."

The woman turned to Clyde. "Thank you again, sir. I really appreciate this."

"Glad to help. You take care now."

They left the woman climbing into her car and walked toward the restaurant.

"Well, that was weird." Martha grinned up at Clyde. "What do you think? Was her story legit?"

He shrugged. "Who knows?"

"Well, if it wasn't, she sure was a good actress. I believed her."

"Yep." Clyde nodded. "You fell for her, hook, line, and sinker. You really put me on the spot, too, when you said we'd give her a twenty. What was I going to say? 'No'?" Frowning, he opened the door and ushered her inside. "Let's go eat."

The hostess seated them, and they unfolded their menus.

Martha's eyes met Clyde's. "I'd still rather be too trusting than cynical all the time." She watched his expression.

He ignored her remark and studied the menu.

Martha continued. "But I'll have to admit that part about her being a policeman's widow with no friends or family to call was a little much."

Clyde looked up. "You got that right. And what about hitting a deer and having her purse stolen all in one morning?" He scowled. "Man! She had her story down pat, didn't she? Even approached us with a road map in her hand to throw us off guard. I bet she stops at places all up and down the interstate here."

Martha nodded. "And the crazy thing is she's bound to get only a ten or twenty each time. Maybe she gets her real kicks out of seeing how many people she can con. I'm sure most people are like us, though. They hate to say no to someone like that."

"I wish now I'd taken a look at her license plate," Clyde said. "Maybe the next fellow will be more observant."

A waitress came to take their order, and they dropped their discussion.

After lunch, they exited the restaurant, turned the corner of the building—and stopped.

"Oh, my gosh." Martha grabbed Clyde's arm. "There she is. I thought for sure she'd be long gone by now."

"You're right! Talk about pressing your luck! Well, that dame is crazier than she looks if she thinks I'm going to let her hang around here and con some other poor sucker." Clyde whipped out his cell. "This time I'm calling a cop."

He punched the nine-one-one button on his phone, reported the incident, and the two of them stood on the porch and waited. When the patrol car arrived, Clyde directed it toward the woman's car.

Martha watched the officer pull in behind her. A tall, hefty policeman stepped out, adjusted his belt and holster, and moved toward the car. For a moment, he stood by the open window and talked. Then he returned to his vehicle with something in his hand. Couldn't be the woman's driver's license if her purse was stolen.

The police radio crackled, but Martha couldn't make out any words. Then the officer turned and waved in their direction.

Puzzled, she and Clyde moved toward the car. The woman opened her door, stood and greeted them with a smile. "Hi, there. I've been waiting for you."

She stuck out the twenty-dollar bill. "I won't need this, but you were so kind to give it to me. My name is Angela Hawthorne, and I'm a graduate student at Vanderbilt University in Nashville."

Clyde retrieved the money and reached for his wallet.

Martha frowned. "You're a student?"

"Yes, I'm a graduate student in the Sociology Department. The subject of my dissertation is benevolence, but I'm especially interested in the willingness of people to give aid to a stranger. You and your husband were part of an experiment. My hypothesis is that the majority of people will respond positively to help someone in distress, even when uncertain. Your actions today support my hypothesis." She smiled and offered her hand. "Thank you, again."

Clyde grinned and gave her a vigorous handshake. "We were glad to help, but you're right about us being uncertain." He laughed. "We've been second-guessing ourselves ever since we left you."

"Most people do," Angela said. "My story was full of holes, but your first instinct was to help, and that overcame your doubts."

Martha glanced at the officer jotting notes on his clipboard. "Do most people call the police?"

"A few, but I obtained permission from state law enforcement and the Cracker Barrel managers before I carried out this experiment. Everyone has been most kind."

"Well, good luck with your dissertation," Clyde said. "It's an interesting hypothesis, and your paper should be fascinating."

Martha nodded and smiled at Angela. "He's right, but I *will* have to say, if you ever want to pursue another career, Broadway is waiting."

Author's note: ENCOUNTER

On a trip to visit our children in Franklin, Tennessee, my husband and I stopped at a Cracker Barrel restaurant outside Memphis. We stepped out of our car, and a middle-aged woman approached us. Her tale was exactly the same as the one the woman told to Clyde and Martha. We, too, fell for it "hook, line and sinker," and Robin gave her a twenty-dollar bill. We still do not know if the real woman's story about her stolen purse was true or not. We never saw her again.

When writing fiction, it's fun to use a personal experience, change the characters, and give the story a new twist. How could Clyde and Martha learn whether or not their second-guessing was correct? I pondered this for several days. Then early one morning, an idea for a plausible outcome came to mind. I was glad to give my story a happier ending.

In September 2011 at the White County Creative Writers' Conference, "Encounter" won third place in the Writer's Choice short story, fiction, any genre contest sponsored by Fiction Writers of Central Arkansas.

Chigger Lessons

"Listen up, children." Mama Chigger teetered on one leg and waved her seven other feet to get attention. "The lessons you learn today can mean the difference between life and death."

All squirming stopped. Every little eye turned in her direction.

"As newly hatched larvae, you must now go out into the world and earn your keep. Your job is to stake out your prey and then move quickly to obtain nourishment."

Louie Larva nudged his brother and grinned. "That sounds like fun."

Mama frowned. "Well, remember this, young man. Eating is very serious business. How well you execute these procedures will determine your destiny."

With a dramatic flourish, Mama descended from her leafy podium. "Step back now, children. We are about to begin Lesson Number One: How to Identify the Victim."

The mother mite danced in the dust, twirling and spinning left to right as she dragged one toe to trace a large figure on the ground. The shape of a head emerged and then a body with two arms and two long legs.

At last, Mama paused to catch her breath. Then she continued. "These giant creatures are called *humans*. With thundering steps they invade our territory. Fortunately, we members of the chigger kingdom are almost invisible. Humans cannot see us."

As if on cue, crashing sounds interrupted the lesson.

"That's one of your targets now," Mama said. "The giant who lives in this house comes into the yard to work in her flower beds. Now that spring is here, she will be eager to get outside. This will be your best time to attack. We chiggers hibernate all winter, buried in the ground, so humans become less cautious. You larvae children must now be ready to proceed where we left off last summer."

Memories of youth flooded Mama's mind. Gone were the happy days of suckling. This year she would forage in the dirt for sustenance.

"Most humans think we adults are the ones who attack, but they're wrong. It's you little larvae who will enjoy the feast." Mama swept her legs out in a magnanimous gesture toward her young listeners.

The children whistled and cheered.

Louie Larva stepped forward. "Can we eat the human now?"

"Not yet. She'll be moving this way in a moment. You must now learn Lesson Number Two: How to Attack."

She pointed again to the figure she had drawn.

"These lower extremities will be your points of entry. Humans wear hard things on their feet—they call them shoes—but above the cloth around their ankles you can pounce onto their skin. Under those coverings are sweaty areas that are very tasty. The skin is thin there, and you can suck the juices easily."

Louie smacked his lips. "Sounds yummy."

Mama continued. "But that's not all. If you want to find an extra delicious spot, you can skitter up the leg to a soft, fleshy fold behind the knee or even farther up to a tender, moist area where the leg joins the body." She indicated the spot on the outline and sighed. "I remember how warm and sweet that crease was. You can rest there for as long as you like. It's only after you're gone that the bite will get red and itchy. Then the human will scratch and bellow. Her noisy complaints will be frightening, so you'll need to hurry home as fast as you can. Your belly will be full, but you'll be feeling no pain."

The children's eyes sparkled. "We're starving. Can we go now?"

"You'll have your chance soon. Here she comes. Remember now, be careful. Jump high and hold on. Then scoot up as far as you can. It'll be dark, but find a juicy spot. You won't be disappointed."

Mama Chigger laughed as her offspring sprinted toward the giant.

These first delightful days of spring were always the best times for feeding. Later, humans sprayed their skin with slimy, smelly goop to ward off an attack. Then it would be more difficult to get a good bite, although it could still be done if a chigger held his breath and scrambled to an uncoated spot.

She would teach that lesson tomorrow. Today her children's maiden voyage onto fresh flesh should be a celebration of wild abandonment and joy—a delicious time to remember forever.

"Bon appetit, my darlings. Bon appetit."

Author's note: CHIGGER LESSONS

The first summer after we moved to Arkansas, we met many of Mama Chigger's children. They feasted for days on their juicy targets before we realized what was happening.

Later, I ran across Mama Chigger coaching her offspring, and I vowed to expose her secrets. No innocent human should ever again be caught unaware!

In March 2008 "Chigger Lessons" won second place in a Village Writers' Club contest. In May of that year, I read this tale at our club's annual L'Audible Art event when we writers shared our stories, poems, and essays with an appreciative audience.

Amanda's Secret

We stood in shadows on the porch, and I kissed Mandy goodnight. Behind us, the front door opened, revealing a pajama-clad boy about seven, sporting a mischievous grin.

"Hi, Mom."

Mandy froze in my arms and then whirled around. "Jamie, what are you doing up? Where's Tina?"

"She's watching TV."

"Well, you need to be in bed."

Mandy pushed back the door and hustled the child into the living room. "I'm sorry, Joe. Come on in. I'll need to get him settled."

I stepped from the porch into the room and closed the door behind me.

"Jamie, this is Mr. Collins, the man who works with me downtown. Joe, this is Jamie, a very smart boy who's in *big* trouble right now." She raised her eyebrows and cast a stern look in her son's direction.

I smiled at the freckled face beaming up at me. "Hi, Jamie. I think your mom means business."

"Yeah, I know. But I just wanted to say 'Goodnight.'" He crossed his arms and faked a pout.

Mandy patted him on his shoulder. "Well, say 'Goodnight' then, and we'll head for bed."

"Goodnight, mister. See ya." He marched down the hall with Mandy behind.

I looked around and settled into an easy chair. Wall shelves beside me contained a few books and some photographs of Jamie. One picture showed Mandy and Bob building a sand castle with Jamie on the beach. All three wore sunglasses as they smiled into the camera.

A teen-aged girl strolled into the room, and I stood to greet her. "Hi, there. You must be Tina. I'm Joe. Jamie and his mom are back in the bedroom. He met us at the front door."

"He did?" She laughed. "That little rascal. I put him to bed an hour ago."

"He's tricky," said Mandy, reentering the room, "but maybe he's down for the night now." She paid the sitter, thanked her, and Tina was on her way.

Mandy and I moved to the couch. "Guess by now you're ready to call it a night." I smiled, caressing her face. Her soft brown eyes looked tired as I brushed a strand of hair from her cheek.

"Joe, I had a good time. But we need to take it slow, okay? I know, we've been dating a month, and it's been fun, but I'm really not ready for anything serious right now." She sighed and rested her head against the back of the couch. "You can see how hard it is on Jamie if I'm gone too much at night. It's only been a year since Bob died, and he still needs me around."

"I understand that, darling. I won't rush you. We can take our time." I patted her hand, pulled her close, and kissed her lightly on the forehead. "Just give us a chance. You're such a beautiful woman and a very smart lady. I'd be a fool to let you get away."

She smiled, turned up her face for another kiss, and then gently pushed me away. "Joe, you're a great guy. You make me feel good. But I think you'd better go now. I'll see you again in the morning."

She stood and pulled me up beside her. "You think you know me, but there are things I haven't told you. It will be a long time before I can reveal all my secrets." She sounded serious.

"Well, Ms. Amanda Morgan, I'm game for whatever skeletons you pull out of your closet. You won't be able to scare me off that easily."

She laughed, and we walked to the door and said our good-byes. Sliding behind the wheel, I slipped my key into the ignition and backed into the street.

People at work said she and Bob had a good marriage. I thought about how he died—spinning out of control, crossing the median, plowing into that semi.

This had been a tough year, but Mandy seemed to be doing well. She was a strong woman. I hoped it wouldn't be long before she trusted me enough to keep her secrets safe.

The next day at ten, we met in the company break room. I pulled a chair to her table.

"Joe, I'm sorry about last night." She avoided my eyes and stirred her coffee.

"No problem. Whatta you say we plan an outing on Saturday? We can bring Jamie along."

A smiled flickered. "What do you have in mind?"

"Well, how about …"

"Oh, my God! It's Jamie." With a look of horror, she grabbed my arm.

"What?"

"He's running into the street."

She jumped up and dashed through the door. "Joe, I've got to go. Tell them I've got to go."

I chased her down the hall. She rushed into her office, grabbed her purse from the cabinet, and took off out into the parking lot.

"Mandy, I'm coming too. Give me your keys."

Confused, she fumbled inside her bag, and I snatched it from her, produced the keys, and jumped into the driver's seat. She ran to the passenger side and hopped in.

"Where to? Where's Jamie?" My mind raced.

"At home. Oh, my God, it's too late." She broke down, huge sobs wracking her body.

I wheeled the car onto her street. Blue and red flashing lights greeted us. A police car and ambulance blocked her driveway, and a small crowd of neighbors huddled on the sidewalk. A short distance away, officers talked with a distraught-looking man.

"Jamie!" She leaped from the car as I pulled to the curb.

Views from an Empty Nest

I parked and ran to her. She clutched Jamie's hand as the child lay motionless on a gurney, a neck brace supporting his head. Two attendants hovered over him. An older woman stood nearby, crying quietly.

"He's going to be fine." The paramedic's calm voice sounded reassuring. "Looks like a mild concussion with a few bumps and bruises, but his pulse is strong, and he's breathing fine."

"Thank God." Mandy sank to the ground.

I dropped beside her and wrapped her in my arms.

The other woman moved closer. "I'm so sorry, Amanda. He was out the door before I knew it."

Mandy looked up and nodded, but she didn't speak.

Later, attendants helped her into the ambulance, and I drove behind them to the hospital, parked in the visitors' lot, and entered the ER waiting room. I glanced around. Young and old sprawled on couches and chairs in rows down the middle and along the walls.

Mandy emerged from a hallway and moved toward me. "Everything seems to be all right. They'll admit him overnight for observation. Joe, thank you for being here."

I took her in my arms. "I'm so sorry this happened to Jamie and you."

Looking up, her eyes met mine. "I saw it coming, Joe. That's my 'secret.' I can see when something bad is about to happen."

"That must be awful."

"It only happens with those I love, but you're right—it's awful. I can't do anything to stop it. I saw Bob's crash right before he lost control."

Tears brimmed again, and I steered her toward an empty couch. "I'm glad to be with you, Mandy. I'll always be with you."

She nestled beside me and leaned her head on my shoulder. Soon the doctors would call her to be with Jamie, but for now, at least for a moment, I could offer my comfort.

Someday I'll tell my darling I have a secret too. Will she believe me? Maybe not, but it won't really matter. I'll be with my beautiful wife and son again, and this time our lives will go on—forever.

Author's note: AMANDA'S SECRET

Stories set in a world of make-believe and supernatural events have always been popular. "Amanda's Secret" was my first attempt in fantasy fiction, and I enjoyed creating this tale dealing with the paranormal.

In June 2008 the original piece won second place in the Grand Conference Award for Fiction at Arkansas Writers' Conference. That contest called for the first three pages of a novel or short story, beginning with the words, "The door opened behind her, revealing a …"

Later, I revised the beginning slightly and completed the story. On March 22, 2010, "Amanda's Secret" won first place in a Village Writers' Club contest for Fantasy.

Ghost Story

From a first-floor window, Deputy Jasper Franklin watched the crowd gathering on the courthouse lawn. At straight-up nine, he unlocked the front entrance and moved to one side as visitors poured into the lobby and wound their way up the creaky wooden staircase to the second floor.

He stood erect, in full uniform, but there'd be no need to swipe anyone with the metal detector today. Young and old streamed by his station to hand him their tickets, and he greeted each one with a smile. The tale these folks came to hear would curl their toes. People loved a mystery, especially a good ghost story like this one.

When all were inside, he closed the door, made his way up the stairs, and took his seat in the back of the courtroom.

Up front, his friend called for everyone's attention. "Good morning, ladies and gentlemen. Welcome to Cloward County. This is the tenth year we have hosted storytelling sessions at our historic courthouse, and the mystery is still as fresh as ever. My name is Sam Lawton, and I'm the founder and manager of a company called Paranormal Investigators. We look into reports of unusual occurrences—spirit sightings, voices from the dead, all kinds of psychic phenomena—to verify their authenticity."

Sam paused and surveyed the crowd. His listeners sat motionless, ready.

"As of today, P-I has investigated at least a dozen cases here in Cloward County—people claiming they've encountered the ghost of a man named Joshua Jacob Clark. Most of the sightings have been right here on these premises. We've brought in our cameras, infrared lights, and other recording devices to collect evidence. And ladies and gentlemen, I'm here to tell you, it's absolutely true. The spirit of Joshua Jacob Clark is alive and well."

A murmur passed through the audience, and an elderly couple in front of Jasper nodded to each other and smiled.

Deputy Franklin knew the story by heart, but he still loved to hear Sam tell it. His friend had been entertaining crowds like this once a month for years, and no question about it, all the folks in Cloward County reaped the rewards. People came from all around, even from out of state. Restaurants and motels did a booming business, not to mention Jasper himself. Each month he collected a nice little paycheck from the P-I group for helping out. Yes, sir, as far as he was concerned, Joshua Jacob Clark could haunt this place as long as he liked.

Storyteller Sam smiled at the crowd's reaction. He moved away from the lectern, took a sip of water from a glass on the table and then began his narrative.

"Joshua Jacob Clark was a black man who lived in this county back in the 1930s. He was a strong, young fellow, a hard worker, and he and his folks sharecropped out on the Benson place. But Joshua made a big mistake one day. He stepped out of line and spoke to a young lady by the name of Genevieve Parsons when they passed each other on the street. In those days, no black man would dare to approach a white woman in such a bold manner. That was considered an affront to gentility and social custom. Miss Genevieve was the daughter of Mayor Andrew Parsons, and she came home and told her daddy that Clark frightened her."

Some in the audience began to squirm. Jasper smiled. There were always a few who seemed to foresee what was coming.

"The next night, Miss Genevieve spotted someone lurking outside her window—watching her undress, she said. She pointed the finger at young Clark. The mayor called the sheriff, and it wasn't long till a posse rounded up Clark and brought him in for questioning. He denied being near the Parsons' house—swore he'd been in a honky-tonk ten miles from there and witnesses could vouch for him. But a black man's word didn't count for much in those days. They arrested him for trespassing and slapped him in jail."

Sam paused, cleared his throat, and took another sip of water—mostly to heighten the suspense, Jasper thought.

"The KKK was an active group back then, and a few days later, a mob broke into the Cloward County Jail and dragged Clark out to that big oak in front of the courthouse. They strung him up right there on the spot. Next day, the newspaper account, dated May 24, 1937, seemed to condone the lynching—'a potential rapist getting his just reward,' it said. Today, some people claim the ghost of Joshua Jacob Clark still haunts these premises because he's angry—angry at the injustice and angry that he, an innocent man, was killed."

A tall, bald fellow in the second row raised his hand. "Mr. Lawton, you said sightings of Clark's spirit have been verified. Explain what you've got."

"You bet." Sam stepped to one side, picked up a screen and placed it in front of the judge's bench. He pointed to Jasper in the back. "Deputy Franklin, how about cutting those lights now, and we'll show these good folks some slides."

While Jasper flipped switches, Sam moved to a projector in the middle of the room and clicked it on. A blurry black-and-white image flickered in the dark room.

"Here is one picture of what we believe is Clark's spirit," Sam said, adjusting the lens. "This was taken in the courthouse attic last year. Marlene Kirkpatrick, one of our most experienced investigators, spent the night to check out disturbances reported by a secretary in the county clerk's office. Miss Kirkpatrick verified the noises—low groaning sounds, like someone in pain—and she noted a cool breeze swept through the room two times, although there are no outside openings in the attic. Using her infrared camera, she captured a hazy apparition moving beneath the rafters."

Sam stepped closer to the picture and pointed a lighted arrow at the photo. "You can see a shadowy figure there on the right side."

People leaned forward, moving left and right to get a better view.

"Excuse me, Mr. Lawton." A woman's voice rang out in the darkness. "My name is Gloria Wilson. That young lady in your story, Genevieve Parsons, was my grandmother. May I speak to the group?"

Framed in the dusty beam, Sam looked startled. "Of course. Jasper, let's have some lights again."

Sam moved to shut off the projector, the room brightened, and all eyes focused on an attractive woman in a red sweater standing near the front.

"All right, miss. Please go ahead," Sam said.

"Thank you. I drove down from Springfield to attend today's presentation. Recently, my mother, Arlene Wilson, passed away. In her lock box, we discovered a journal that belonged to her mother, my grandmother, Genevieve Parsons Brown. What is in this diary will be of interest to all of you, I'm sure." She lifted a small, leather-bound book for all to see.

"Absolutely, Ms. Wilson. What did you find?" Sam appeared to be a bit nervous now as he frowned and took another sip of water from the glass on the table.

"After Joshua Clark was hanged, my grandmother must have suffered tremendous guilt. She knew she couldn't be sure the man looking in her window was Joshua, and the sorrow she felt after his death was overwhelming. I don't know if young Joshua Jacob Clark is still haunting this courthouse or not, but his spirit certainly haunted my Grandmother Genevieve until the day she died."

Silence fell over the crowd, and Jasper shifted in his seat.

The speaker continued. "Here, let me read you an entry posted the day after Clark's death. It's dated May 24, 1937, the same date you gave for the newspaper clipping."

Gloria Wilson slipped on her reading glasses, opened the book to a marked page, and began.

Dear Diary,

Today has been the most horrible day of my life. Joshua Jacob Clark, a Negro who worked for James Benson, was hanged on the courthouse square last night. Daddy says he got what he deserved. Now I'm afraid Daddy and some of his friends may have done the killing. I cannot bear to think of it. A man is dead because of me. I told Daddy it might have been Joshua at my window, but I didn't say I knew for sure. Dear God, forgive me.

Ms. Wilson paused, removed her glasses, folded them, and looked around at the crowd. "In a later entry, Genevieve mentioned that one of the Benson boys—Howard—had a crush on her. She wondered if it could have been him who visited her that night. Of course, my grandmother never revealed any of these thoughts to her family, and when my mother inherited the journal, she never told any of us children about it, either. But I do think it's time for the truth to come out, don't you?"

For a moment, Sam seemed at a loss for words. When he regained his composure, he smiled. "Thank you, Ms. Wilson. Your grandmother's diary seems to corroborate what many people have been thinking for a long time."

From the front, a scattering of applause began and spread across the room until all were standing, clapping, and cheering.

Jasper rose and joined in the celebration. But a nagging thought entered his mind. What if this new evidence caused their resident Cloward County ghost to leave? Without his regular moans and appearances, these monthly money-making sessions might very well come to an end.

On the other hand, Clark's family could finally rejoice if all doubts about his innocence were put to rest. Surely that would be a good thing—for everyone.

Behind the last row of chairs, a wispy breeze stirred, brushed the back of Jasper's neck, and gently ruffled his hair.

Author's note: GHOST STORY

Readers and writers often ask how I come up with new story ideas. I have found interesting newspaper articles to be an excellent source.

On September 14, 2009, a headline in our Hot Springs, Arkansas, paper, the *Sentinel-Record*, caught my attention: "Ghost Hunters Seek Spirit of Lynched Arkansas Man."

The article said historic newspaper accounts and courthouse documents revealed how a band of twenty-five Sharp County men broke into the Lawrence County Jail at Powhatan before dawn on May 21, 1887, and hanged Andrew Springer from a tree. Paranormal investigators believed Springer's spirit still haunted the old Powhatan Courthouse that sat near the jail and tree where he was hanged.

"This building is one of the most haunted places in Arkansas," said Spirit Seekers investigative director, Alan L. "Buz" Lowe.

According to the article, Spirit Seekers, a not-for-profit organization, investigated hauntings throughout Arkansas. The group studied the courthouse for several years after investigators said they found Andrew's spirit roaming the attic and jail. Springer, a black man accused of raping a white woman in Sharp County, was transferred to Lawrence County in an attempt to protect him from a mob like the one that killed him.

I found it fascinating that modern-day ghost hunters investigated paranormal events, especially hauntings believed to be caused by past racial injustice. I used that theme to spin this new "Ghost Story."

The Lion's Den

"Hi, Mom." Betty Jean burst into the kitchen and gave her mother a quick hug. "You won't believe the crowd at school this morning—all those National Guard guys everywhere—looked like we were going to war. I'm hungry. Do we have any more of Clara's cake left?"

At the sink, Betty Jean's mother frowned, wiped her hands on a towel, and turned toward her daughter. "There's still some cake under that lid. I've been worried about you. That uppity NAACP was determined to go ahead with their plans, no matter what our governor said or did."

Betty Jean helped herself to a giant wedge of yesterday's dessert. "Yeah. If the Negro students showed up, we never saw them. The Guard must have kept them out. All us kids were inside, but we watched everything from Mr. Anderson's windows upstairs. He said this was 'history in the making,' so he didn't try to do much teaching." She pulled a bottle of milk from the refrigerator, poured a glass, and carried her snack to the table.

Mother pulled out a chair and sat beside Betty Jean. "Well, it's terrible the way those Negroes insist on stirring things up. They have their own schools, for heaven's sake. You remember Clara's daughter, Ruby. She's doing just fine. In fact, Clara was bragging on her—said Ruby made all A's last year. Maybe you need to stay home tomorrow. I don't want you mixed up in all that."

"We'll be okay. The Guard is protecting us. They lined up all around the school and only let us students and teachers get through." Betty Jean took another bite of cake, drank a swallow of milk, and continued. "Most of those other people out there weren't from around here. At least, I didn't see anyone I knew."

Mother nodded. "They're coming from all around Little Rock, I guess. People don't want to integrate, and they'll do whatever they can to stop it. Clara told me today that Ruby's best friend, Elizabeth Eckford, was selected to enroll at Central. Her parents must have agreed, but it sure will be dangerous."

Betty Jean wiped her mouth with a napkin. "Well, I'm glad Clara's not pushing Ruby to get involved in all that stuff."

Half an hour later, the phone rang, and Betty Jean ran to answer it. Maybe it was Alice, calling to report who was in all her classes. The high-pitched voice on the other end surprised her.

"Betty Jean, this is Ruby. Were you at school today?"

"Sure, it was the first day. Why wouldn't I be?" Betty Jean frowned.

"Well, I was afraid you might have stayed home. I really, really need your help with something. Can you meet me somewhere?"

"What's the matter? I can't just go running out for no reason."

"I need you to talk to my friend. She's planning to go to Central tomorrow, and I have to get her to stop."

Betty Jean paused. "If she won't listen to you, what makes you think she'll listen to me?"

"'Cause you were there today. You saw all those soldiers and that mob out there. She thinks she'll be protected, but she's gonna get hurt, I just know it."

"You're right. Why are her parents making her do it?"

"I don't know. It's crazy. But we gotta get her to quit. Please, please help me, Betty Jean, pul-leeze?"

Ruby's shrill, whiny voice made Betty Jean cringe. "I guess I can talk to her, but I doubt if it'll do any good. Where do you want me to meet you? I can't be gone long."

"Oh, thank you, thank you. I'll get Elizabeth, and we'll meet you out back in thirty minutes."

The line went dead, and Betty Jean returned the receiver to its cradle. When Ruby was little, she'd come with her mother to work sometimes, and she and Betty Jean would play. Ruby would freak out over the silliest things—like that time when Picasso, their cat, delivered a dead mouse on the doorstep and Ruby screamed to high heaven. You'd have thought the mouse had run right up her leg. Betty Jean giggled, remembering Ruby's reaction. Now they were both fifteen. This time Ruby had good reason to be scared.

On the back porch, Betty Jean moved back and forth in the old wooden swing. Late afternoon shadows played across the floor. A ceiling fan lazily stirred the air. Why did it always have to be so hot during the first weeks of school? Little Rock wouldn't be cool until October. Then she and Alice could wear their new cashmere sweaters. Going to football games would be more fun too. It was hard to root for your team when your blouse stuck to your back and sweat ran down your legs.

At last, Ruby and her friend emerged from the alley, and Betty Jean stepped out to greet them.

Ruby spoke first. "Betty Jean, this is Elizabeth. She didn't want to come, but I told her you'd be her friend."

The girl stood there, motionless. She stared at Betty Jean through horn-rimmed glasses.

Betty Jean smiled. "I'm pleased to meet you, Elizabeth. Ruby and I have known each other a long time."

Elizabeth blinked. "Ruby says you want to talk to me about Central." Her flat tone matched the deadpan look on her face.

"Yeah. I'm sure you already know how most folks feel about you going there. There's going to be a lot of trouble, and Ruby and I think you need to stay home tomorrow—for your own safety."

Elizabeth glanced over at Ruby and then glared at Betty Jean. "Well, it's too late to back out now. There are nine of us going, and we'll stick together. Besides, Mrs. Daisy Bates will help us. She's president of the Arkansas Chapter of the National Association for the Advancement of Colored People, and she says its time for us to stand up for our rights. After all, it's been three years since the Supreme Court ruled that segregation in the schools was unconstitutional."

Betty Jean frowned. Elizabeth's spirited response surprised her. "That may be true, but it'll be a lot more years before Negroes are accepted in the white schools around here. We just don't want you to get hurt, that's all."

"I know. But sometimes, people have to take a chance and do what's right." Elizabeth grabbed Ruby's arm. "Come on, let's go."

Ruby's eyes filled with tears. "You're just so stubborn, Elizabeth. Betty Jean saw all those mean people out there today. You'll be walking right into the lion's den."

"Maybe so. But the Lord protected Daniel, didn't he? We'll be okay. It was nice to meet you, Betty Jean. Maybe I'll see you again some time." Elizabeth turned on her heel and headed toward the alley with Ruby running behind.

Shaking her head, Betty Jean returned to the house.

The next day, more unruly crowds lined the streets in front of Central High. Once again, uniformed National Guardsmen circled the school. Eager to watch the drama, Betty Jean and her classmates leaned out the open windows in Mr. Anderson's classroom.

One of the boys spoke up. "I saw a group of them a couple blocks away, but I counted only eight. I thought there were supposed to be nine."

"Are you sure there were only eight?" Betty Jean's pulse quickened. Maybe her warnings had helped after all.

"I think so. But there were some older Negroes with them too. Hey, look. Here comes one now—from the other direction." The boy pointed up the street, and Betty Jean turned her head. Oh, no. It was Elizabeth—all alone! What was she doing?

Betty Jean watched the slim figure approach the school as the noisy crowd surged forward. Staring straight ahead, Elizabeth carried a notebook in one arm and kept a steady pace along the sidewalk. Jeers and racial slurs rang out around her. "Go home, nigger. You're not welcome here."

"Yeah, let's lynch this nigger."

A man with a camera jumped out and snapped a photo.

Elizabeth kept right on walking. Betty Jean watched her turn toward the front doors. A guardsman blocked her, and she stopped, pushed up her glasses, then moved back out to the sidewalk as angry spectators yelled and moved in closer. She tried another entrance, and again, a guardsman lifted his rifle with fixed bayonet to block her. Then she disappeared through the crowd down the street.

Betty Jean turned away from the window and sank into her desk. Her eyes stung, and she swallowed a large lump forming in her throat.

The day dragged by. At last, the final bell rang. She made a beeline for the bus, endured the noisy ride home, and rushed into the house.

"Mom? Has Clara called? Elizabeth showed up all by herself. I need to call Ruby and find out what happened." Betty Jean ran to the phone.

Her mother emerged from the kitchen. "What? You don't mean that child tried to enroll all alone? Lord, have mercy. No, Clara hasn't called. She's over at the Pattersons' today."

"What's Clara's number?"

"It's there in the address book. Hurry."

Betty Jean found the number and dialed. The phone rang three times before being answered. "Ruby, you're home. Good. This is Betty Jean. Have you heard from Elizabeth?" Her heart pounded as she pressed the receiver against her ear.

"Yeah. She called me a while ago. She told me she couldn't find the other students at Central this morning, so she caught a bus to go down to where her mother works."

"I know. I saw her. Ruby, it was terrible! Elizabeth had to walk through that mob all by herself for two whole blocks. I'm so glad she's all right."

"Yeah, she told me. People were shouting at her. One lady even spit on her. But she made it down to the corner, and someone helped her get on a city bus."

"Well, it was just like you said. She walked right into the lion's den out there." Betty Jean's voice cracked a little, and she cleared her throat. "But you'd have been so proud of her. I could tell she was scared, but she went right on. I couldn't believe she didn't turn back."

For a moment there was silence. Then Ruby came back on the line. "Betty Jean, Elizabeth is one of the bravest people I know. She knew what she was doing."

Betty Jean paused. "You're right, Ruby. She did."

"Thanks. I'll tell her what you said. See you later, okay?"

Betty Jean hung up the phone and turned toward her mother. "Elizabeth's okay. She caught a bus downtown to where her mother works."

"Well, thank goodness for that. All this integration business is just plain crazy." Shaking her head, Mother left the room.

Betty Jean collapsed onto the couch. The image of that determined figure walking through the angry crowd still burned in her mind. If Elizabeth ever did enroll in Central, she'd face another "lion's den" every single day. Plenty of kids would give her a hard time, and those who befriended her would be called "nigger lovers." Probably get the same treatment as Elizabeth.

Betty Jean wondered if she could stick up for her. To be honest, she wasn't sure.

What was it Elizabeth said? "Sometimes people have to take a chance and do what's right." Maybe so. Sometimes they do. Did she have as much courage as Elizabeth? Guess she'd just have to wait and see.

Author's note: THE LION'S DEN

In June 2010 Arkansas Writers' Conference in Little Rock offered a Historical Fiction Award for a short story based on an actual Arkansas historical event. Having lived in the South through the tumultuous struggle for civil rights during the 1950s and 1960s, I decided to set my story during that period.

I had often heard of the bravery of the Little Rock Nine. This group of young black students defied the governor's orders and the National Guard when they marched to integrate Central High School at the beginning of the 1957–1958 school year. One member of the group, Elizabeth Eckford, was photographed as she walked alone through a mob of angry white segregationists. The photo, taken by Will Counts of the *Arkansas Democrat*, propelled the civil rights movement forward in the United States.

"The Lion's Den" relates this dramatic episode exactly as it is documented in historical records. However, the rest of my story is fictional.

"The Lion's Den" won third honorable mention out of sixteen entries in the AWC Historical Fiction contest.

Happy Thanksgiving, Son

The headline on page three caught his attention: "Lack of Body Makes Murder Case Iffy Proposition."

Jerome scanned the article and then leaned back and took another sip of coffee. Things looked good. His mother couldn't be convicted—not without a helluva lot more evidence—and there wasn't any chance of that.

Prosecuting Attorney Doyle Warren told the paper he hoped to put Eleanor Pearson on trial, even if a body wasn't found. The state reported they now had reason to believe she killed her mother, Hilda Hastings, because she became a burden to the family. With the advice of her defense attorney, Jerome's mother pleaded not guilty to Warren's charge of second-degree murder, and without a body, Eleanor was released on fifty thousand dollars' bond.

Four years ago his mother had filed a missing person report. Granny Hastings suffered from Alzheimer's and wandered off. She was never found. Why couldn't Warren accept that? The guy hounded Eleanor every chance he got. Now the pompous ass claimed new evidence indicated Granny had been killed.

Jerome picked up his cell and punched in his mother's number. "Guess you've seen today's paper. What do you think?"

"I think we're still going to be okay. Mr. Andrews says no matter what they say, they can't convict me without a body. I'm going ahead with my plans to prepare Thanksgiving dinner over here next Thursday. We'll celebrate. How about that?" His mother laughed and then broke into a spasm of raspy coughing.

Jerome frowned. Damn cigarettes. He wished she'd listen to her doctor. "Dinner'll be fine," he said. "Don't know if Jack'll be home, though. He told me he'd probably stay down at State for the big game on Friday. What about Carol? Have you heard from her?" His sister usually spent Thanksgiving with her husband's family.

"Nope, but that doesn't surprise me. She's always so busy with all her clubs and charities. Doesn't have time to give her stodgy old mom a call. But I'll check with her this weekend." Eleanor coughed again.

Jerome regretted he'd mentioned Carol. She now lived the good life with that doctor husband of hers. After Granny Hastings got sick, she hadn't lifted a finger to help—just left all the dirty work to him and his mom—caring for Granny 24/7.

When he and Carol were kids and their mom worked, Granny was the one who got them off to school and greeted them when they got home. She was always there for them, cooking their meals, washing their clothes. Even went to all their ball games. After they were grown and Granny started going downhill, you'd have thought Carol never even met the woman.

At work the next morning, Jerome got a call from Doyle Warren. "Mr. Pearson, your girlfriend, Stephanie Chambers, went to the police last week. She claimed you told her what really happened to your grandmother. We need you to come in and give us a statement."

"She's not my girlfriend, damn it. She's my *ex*. You can't believe a word she says. She obtained a protective order against me months ago. I don't know what she told you, but it's bound to be shit."

"We'd like you to come in, Mr. Pearson. The police have new evidence. You may want to get yourself a lawyer."

On Monday before Thanksgiving, Jerome and his lawyer, Thomas Black, met at the courthouse and then made their way upstairs to the office of the prosecuting attorney. The secretary showed them in and introduced them.

Warren sat behind a massive mahogany desk. He rose to shake their hands. "Good afternoon, gentlemen. Thank you for coming in today. Have a seat." He indicated two arm chairs in front of the desk and waited for Jerome and his lawyer to be seated. Then Warren settled into his cushioned leather chair and rolled forward.

"Here's what we've got. On November 9, Miss Stephanie Chambers went to the police. Mr. Pearson, she reported that after your grandmother disappeared, you told Miss Chambers that your mother came to your workplace with a large plastic case and asked you to dispose of it. When you asked what was inside, your mother said, 'Your grandmother.'"

"That's a goddamned lie." Jerome slammed his fist on the desk in front of him.

Attorney Black jumped in. "Mr. Warren, my client will not make any statements or answer any questions. Do the police have a box of remains as evidence?"

"Miss Chambers told the authorities the box was buried behind a barn out on the Hastings property. They've obtained a warrant and are searching, but nothing has been discovered—at least, not yet."

"Well, I think that ends the matter. Is there anything else?"

Leaning forward, Attorney Doyle Warren folded thick hands on top of the desk and fixed steely eyes on Jerome. "Yes, I plan to request that your client not be allowed to visit with his mother from now until the trial. We don't want them corroborating their stories."

"That will require a court order," Black said. "Besides, we don't even know if the case against Eleanor Pearson will go to trial. With only the word of a disgruntled ex-girlfriend against the word of my client and his mother, you know that's not enough evidence to bring this before a jury."

"Just giving you a heads-up, Mr. Black. We'll let the judge make that decision." Warren stood, extended his hand and ushered them out.

As expected, the superior court judge denied the request to keep Jerome away from his mother. On Thursday he drove to her home for the holiday.

Jerome strolled into the kitchen and draped his arm around his mother's stooped shoulders. "Guess it's just you and me today, kid." He grinned. The pungent aroma of cornbread dressing filled the room. "We're a good team, Mom. Can I help you fix anything?"

"Yeah, you can stir this gravy. It's about time to take out the dressing." Eleanor picked up two potholders, bent over, and removed the steaming dish from the oven. Setting it on the back of the stove, she moved to one side so Jerome could grab the spoon.

Views from an Empty Nest

While Jerome stirred, she sat at the kitchen table and lit a cigarette. "Your sister called yesterday. She saw the article in the newspaper." His mother blew smoke toward the ceiling. "Said she was glad they admitted an impending trial was doubtful."

"You're damn right. There's no way they can go to trial. Even if they do, they'll never prove anything. There's no evidence of murder. You just did what you had to do. When Granny got hold of that pistol, you had to get it away from her. I'm just sorry I wasn't here. If I could've distracted her, she might have dropped it."

Eleanor nodded, took another puff, and laid her cigarette in the ash tray. "I didn't mean to shoot her, but I can't say I'm sorry. Can't say I'm sorry I burned her body, either. You know she wasn't herself anymore—just a shell."

"I know." Jerome glanced at his mother. "Granny was a handful, poor thing. Pulling off her clothes, roaming all over the house during the night. You never got a good night's sleep."

"Yeah, I think we have a lot to be thankful for, don't you? Granny's no longer suffering, and we've had four good years now since she 'wandered away.'" Eleanor smiled and picked up her cigarette. "Happy Thanksgiving, son."

Jerome looked around. "Where's the turkey, Mom?"

"The turkey?"

"Yeah, did you bake a turkey?"

His mother blinked. "I … I don't know." She gave Jerome a puzzled look, then stepped over and opened the oven door. "No, it's not in here. Oh, dear. I must have forgot."

Author's note: HAPPY THANKSGIVING, SON

In 2010 the Maumelle Writers' Conference brochure listed several contests. One called for a fiction short story with the theme, "Thanksgiving at Grandma's house"—a rather bland topic, but one with possibilities, I thought, if I could come up with something unexpected. Maybe I could think of something humorous. Or suspenseful.

Then I remembered another newspaper clipping I had filed. On September 15, 2010, the *Sentinel-Record* published a piece with this provocative headline: "Lack of Body Makes Murder Case Iffy Proposition."

In Burlington, Vermont, prosecutors forged ahead with a murder case against a woman accused of killing her Alzheimer's disease-afflicted mother and then burning the body, even though the remains were never found and there were no eyewitnesses to the killing. The woman had reported her mother as a missing person several years earlier, but she was now being charged in her mother's death after an informant said the elderly woman had been killed.

I decided to use this true-life event to spin my tale, and I gave it an even more bizarre twist at the end.

In November 2010 "Happy Thanksgiving, Son" received first honorable mention in the Maumelle contest. I was also excited when the story took first place in a Village Writers' Club short story contest in December.

Unexpected Gifts

"Where on earth is this place? Surely no one lives this far out in the boonies." Velma leaned forward, clutching the wheel of her late-model Lexus. The dirt road was a challenge.

"Well, these are the directions they gave us." Pauline studied the sheet in front of her. "It says this family lives four-and-a-half miles past Cedar Creek Road, and we crossed that a while ago. It shouldn't be too much farther."

"I sure hope not." Velma glanced at her friend. Pauline stared straight ahead, frowning.

"Did you deliver Christmas gifts last year?" Velma asked.

Pauline nodded. "Charlotte and I went, but that family lived just outside of town. This one must be new on our list."

The car rounded a bend. Off to their right, a trailer stood in a grove of pines. "There, that must be it." Velma slowed, turned into the dirt driveway, and cut off the engine. "What a mess!"

Scraps of wood and pieces of corrugated tin littered the yard. Beside the trailer a rusted cab of an abandoned truck sat among tall weeds. Another old pickup was parked near a shed.

"Even if they're poor, I can't understand why people want to live like this." Velma shook her head in disgust. "Seems like they'd have more pride."

The two women climbed out of the car and made their way over to the small porch. At the top of the steps, Velma knocked on the door.

Opening it just a crack, a middle-aged woman peered out. Wispy hair framed her lined face. "What do you want?" she asked.

"We're here from the Covington Women's Club in town." Velma smiled. "We have some Christmas gifts for you and your family."

"We didn't ask for no help." The ungracious response caught Velma off guard.

Pauline's cheerful voice filled the void. "That's okay. We'd still like you to have some food and other things to brighten your holidays."

The woman opened the door wider. "Sam and I don't need nothin'. I guess the kids could use some stuff, though. Of course, they know there's no Santa or nothin', but they hear all the other kids at school talkin' about presents."

"Well, we have a few gifts for each of them," Pauline said. "And there is a box of food. Is there someone else here who could help us unload the car?"

The woman turned and hollered back into the trailer. "Sam, come out here. Some folks are here with some food and stuff."

A scruffy-bearded man in overalls appeared beside her.

"Mr. Bowman?" Velma said.

"That's me." The man squinted at her with cold, blue eyes.

"Mr. Bowman, our Covington Women's Club received your family's name from the counselor at school. She thought you might enjoy having some extra things for your children at Christmas."

"Lady, I'm sorry. We don't know nothin' about this. We don't take charity." He scowled at the two women.

Velma glanced at Pauline.

The man looked over at his wife and then back at the women. He scratched his head. "But seein' as how you're already here, I guess we can oblige you." He stepped out onto the porch. "I'll carry whatever you've got."

"The food is in the trunk." They moved toward the car, and Velma pressed the opener on her key ring.

"That's a lot of stuff there," Sam said. Leaning over, he hoisted the box of canned goods, cereals, and other staples onto the rim of the trunk and then lifted it and carried it into the house.

"We can get some of the other things," said Velma. She and Pauline retrieved the gifts from the back seat. The presents were tagged with the children's names: Alice, age twelve; Jeremy, age nine; Jesse, age eight; and

Cassie, age six. A box of clothing had also been collected. They deposited everything in the trailer's front room.

Looking around, Sam shook his head. "This is a lot of stuff," he announced again. "Like I said, we don't usually ask for no handouts. We get along just fine. But you can tell your folks we 'preciate it."

"We will." Velma forced a smile. "We hope all of you have a very merry Christmas."

Back in the car, she took a deep breath. "Whew, that was weird! I wasn't sure they were even going to take what we brought."

"Yeah, you'd think they'd have been more excited." Pauline frowned. "Guess we really must have caught them by surprise."

Bouncing along the rutted road, the women headed back the way they had come. Heavy silence hung between them.

Velma glanced at the rearview mirror. A pickup approached fast, headlights flashing.

"Well, guess what? I think our friendly Mr. Bowman is after us."

Pauline turned to look. "You're right. That's the truck that was parked in their yard."

Velma slowed and pulled over near the ditch. "Wonder if he's decided not to take the gifts after all."

The truck screeched to a halt behind them. The man stepped out and ambled toward the car. Velma pressed the button to roll down the window.

Leaning over, Sam's face broke into a smile as he peered into the car. "I'm glad I caught you. Back there, when you was gettin' stuff out of your car, you must have dropped your purse. After you left, I looked out there, and this was layin' right where you was parked."

He lifted a brown leather handbag and thrust it through the window.

"Oh, my goodness. Yes, that's mine." Velma reached for her purse. "Thank you so much! I didn't even realize it was gone."

"Figured you'd be missin' it sooner or later. Didn't want you to have to drive all the way back out here again." Now Sam's blue eyes were twinkling.

"You're very kind, Mr. Bowman. I really do appreciate your rushing to bring it to us."

"Well, like I said, I'm glad I caught you. Besides, one good turn deserves another, ain't that right?" Sam laughed.

"I guess so." Velma and Pauline exchanged sheepish grins.

"Merry Christmas, ladies." Sam stepped back. "Y'all take care now." He gave a quick wave, turned, and with a spring in his step, strode back to his truck.

Author's note: UNEXPECTED GIFTS

At Christmas time each year, our Presbyterian Women's organization receives the names of needy families from counselors at local schools. Each PW Circle collects money, and several women in each Circle buy food and gifts for their designated families and deliver the items a few days before the holiday.

However, I have often wondered what it would be like to be the recipient of such charity. Would I be grateful, or would I feel demeaned, knowing I was unable to provide any Christmas gifts for my family? Would I resent wealthy strangers coming to my door, doling out their presents once a year?

We often hear, "It is more blessed to give than to receive." But I think we sometimes forget that *everyone* gets more joy from giving.

I wrote "Unexpected Gifts" to illustrate that point.

A Hundred Thousand Times Better

"Shut up! Just shut your big trap." With eyes burning and fists clenched, Jesse faced his tormentor.

"Well, it's true. You ain't gonna get nothin' from Santa. Your folks is poor, and you ain't even gonna have no tree."

Jesse wanted to clobber him—knock that smug smile off Darrell's face and punch him in the gut. Instead, he spun around and ran. "We already got a tree, you dumb fart!" he yelled over his shoulder. The bully always wanted to fight. Now Jesse just wanted to get away. When Miss Roper rang the recess bell, he was glad to line up and go back to class.

After school Jesse rounded up his two younger sisters, and they headed for home. Scrunching up their shoulders, they shuffled along the dirt road, clutching their jackets around them. Overhead, the pewter sky looked promising. Maybe they'd have snow tonight and no school tomorrow.

"Mama says we got to do our chores before we can play." Mary Ann seemed to delight in bossing her older brother and little sister. Most of the time she rattled on and Jesse paid her no mind, but this afternoon he felt ornery.

"Yeah? Well, guess who gets to bring in the wood this time, Miss Know-It-All? I done it yesterday, so now it's your turn. I'll peel the taters, and Betsy can set the table." Jesse grinned, knowing this would get a rise out of her.

"No way. Mama says toting wood is your job. I ain't gonna bring in no wood."

Jesse laughed. "Mary Ann, you beat all. You know I ain't gonna let you mess with no wood. You ain't strong enough to lift a fly. Mama needs us to have a fire going good tonight."

With that, he took off running, leaving the girls to chase him to the house.

That night in bed Jesse stared at the ceiling. Bitter thoughts of Darrell's taunts nagged at him. It was true. There'd be no Santa this year. With Papa gone, they got by, but Mama didn't earn enough for nothing extra. The girls would be disappointed. He'd have to come up with something. At least, he could get them a tree. They could string some popcorn for chains and find some other stuff for decorations.

The next morning a sprinkling of snow covered the ground. Nothing to get excited about, though. His mama caught a ride with the neighbors into town just like she always did, and a half hour later Jesse and the girls trudged the quarter mile to the schoolhouse.

At recess, Darrell sauntered up to him again.

"Guess your old man won't be coming home for Christmas, will he? My pa says them CCC fellers are working way over in Georgia building bridges and camps and stuff like that. The gov'ment is paying them our tax money."

Jesse glared at Darrell. "Well, at least my pa's working. What's yours doing? Just hanging around McFerrin's, playin' checkers and shootin' the breeze."

"Yeah, and he's got money in the bank too," shot back Darrell. "We done harvested a good crop this year. He says we're gonna have a big Christmas. I'm asking for a Red Ryder BB Gun."

Jesse shrugged. "So, what? When my pa gets home, we'll have lots more money than you. Who cares about Christmas? That's just another day, 'cept we get out of school." Jesse walked away. This time Darrell left him alone.

Saturday before Christmas, Jesse chopped down a small cedar near the ditch by the road, set it in a bucket on the porch, filled it with sand, and dragged it into the house. Then he and the girls trimmed the tree with pine cones, holly berries, and popcorn. That put all of them in a festive mood—Mama too. While they worked on the tree, she sang Christmas carols as she scrubbed their clothes on the washboard at the sink.

"Oh, come all ye faithful,

Joyful and triumphant …"

Jesse smiled. Mama was happy.

On Christmas morning the girls burst into Jesse's room. "Get up, get up. There's snow everywhere." They leaped onto their brother's bed and tugged at his covers.

Betsy pounded on his back. "Santa's come too."

Jesse rolled over. "What did you say?"

"She's right," Mary Ann said. "There's presents under the tree. Hurry. Get up."

In a flash Jesse was out of bed. Grabbing his pants and shirt, he raced into the living room, the girls scampering after him.

Sunlight streamed through the east window, illuminating the decorated tree. Sure enough, three wrapped gifts lay under the branches. Unbelievable!

The girls scrambled to open the packages.

"Wait, wait." Jesse fell to his knees, pushing his sisters to one side. "Let me see the tags."

"This one says 'To Mary Ann.'" Jesse handed the rectangular box to his sister.

"And this one says 'To Jesse.'" He grinned, laying the smaller box beside him. "And this big box says 'To Betsy.'" Her face beaming, his little sister reached for the gift with both hands.

"And this one says 'To my sweetheart.'"

The deep, familiar voice caught them by surprise. Papa walked into the room to lay a tiny box under the tree. Mama stood in the doorway, smiling.

"Papa! Papa!" Jumping up, the children rushed into his outstretched arms. "You're home."

"Yes, I'm home, thank goodness. Merry Christmas, kids. Your mother and I wanted to surprise you, and it looks like we did." He squeezed each of them hard and laughed. "Now go ahead and open your gifts. Let's see what old Santa brought you."

The girls plopped down and tore into their wrappings.

"A pigtail doll!" Mary Ann shouted. "She's beautiful! I love her."

"And I have a baby doll." Betsy lifted her out of the box. "She opens and shuts her eyes!" She tipped her baby forward and back, beaming as the shiny blue eyes and dark lashes fluttered up and down.

"I'm glad old Santa could bring you what you wanted," said Papa. "Son, you can open your box now too."

Jesse sat there with the small package in his lap. Papa was home. That was all that mattered, but he recognized a look of pride on his father's face.

Jesse ripped open the present and stared down at a red knit cap and gloves.

He looked up. Papa was grinning.

"Santa knew you'd need those in this cold, snowy weather."

Jesse managed a smile. "They're great."

"I'm glad you like them. But look, is that a note underneath there?"

Jesse raised the cap and gloves. Opening the folded sheet, he read his father's words:

These will keep you warm while you're using your other gift. I left it on the porch.
Love, Santa.

"Hey! Something's on the porch." Jesse jumped up and dashed for the door. The girls and Mama and Papa were right behind him.

Gleaming in the sunlight bouncing off the snow, a bicycle with royal blue fenders, white racing stripes, and shiny chrome handlebars leaned against the porch railing.

"A bike! Wow! A new bike. This is *really* great." Jesse wrapped his arms around his father's waist.

Papa laughed. "After you get dressed, you can take it for a ride. I'm not sure it'll be easy in this snow, but you can give it a try. We still have one more gift, though. Mama needs to open hers."

The family returned to the tree.

Mama sat on the couch, and Papa kneeled before her, offering his treasure like a prince before a princess. Slowly she untied the ribbon and peeled back the paper.

"Oh, my goodness. Honey, you shouldn't have done this." Tears filled Mama's eyes.

"I don't know why not. You've never had a proper wedding ring. It's time, don't you think?" Papa grinned.

Mama lifted the gold band out of the jewelry box. The tiny diamond glittered as she slipped it onto her finger.

"It's just that money is so tight right now. I don't know what to say."

"How about, 'I love you, darling.'" Papa reached up and gave her a hug. "Don't worry about the money. I've been saving for this a long time."

"Well, it's beautiful. I do love you, darling—so much." Mama gave him a long kiss.

Jesse squirmed as he watched his parents, but he couldn't have been happier. This Christmas had turned out to be the best ever. Papa was home, Mama had a new ring, the girls had new dolls, and he had a *brand new bike*. That was a hundred thousand times better than a stupid old BB gun.

Author's note: A HUNDRED THOUSAND TIMES BETTER

My husband, Robin, grew up in rural Mississippi during the 1930s, and like most folks during the Great Depression, his parents struggled to make ends meet. He was one of eight children, and their Christmas gifts were simple toys, fruits, and nuts.

I thought about Robin's childhood as I created this story about a young boy helping his mother and sisters prepare for Christmas while his father worked for the Civilian Conservation Corps in a nearby state. It was fun to give this story a happy ending.

On December 10, 2007, "A Hundred Thousand Times Better" won first place in the Holiday Story contest sponsored by Village Writers' Club.

Petty Crime

The two edged their way up the driveway toward the house. Dark shadows on the carport hid their faces, but they still wore masks. Inside, the man and woman slept, unaware they were about to become victims of a robbery.

The man rolled over and pushed back the covers. He stood, pausing to get oriented to the darkness, and then moved toward the bathroom. A loud clatter broke the silence, and he jumped.

What was that? Someone trying to get inside? He held his breath and listened. Nothing. Should he investigate? Alert and ready, he eased down the hallway into the den.

There they were—two figures outside the back window. One fellow crouched on the ground, the other on the roof.

The one on top reached down and grabbed the rope with the cedar bird feeder dangling on the end. He pulled it to the roof and pushed off the top. Sunflower seeds spilled down the shingles as the feeder tumbled over the edge.

Those raccoon rascals gobbled that birdseed like two pigs at a trough!

Author's note: PETTY CRIME

During the summer of 2010, the Fine Arts Center in Hot Springs, Arkansas, sponsored their third annual Short Story Writing Competition. Writers were invited to submit a story, two hundred words or less, to be judged by an anonymous panel. The winning stories would be illustrated by local artists and published in an anthology to be sold to raise funds for the Center's art activities.

Eighty-eight stories were submitted, and "Petty Crime" was one of thirty selected for the HSFAC anthology, *Memories and Dreams*. The Center also hosted a reception and book signing on December 16, 2010. Refreshments were served, and winning authors read their stories for the guests.

However, the highlight of the evening came when I unexpectedly received one of three Merit Awards given for stories with the highest scores. The Center presented me with a beautiful certificate and a one-hundred-dollar check, the most money I had ever received in a contest. I was thrilled!

Glory Treasures

Miss Lillian Frances Lancaster leaned forward and peered into the entry's cloudy mirror. Her new hat looked mighty handsome with its silk ribbons and colorful flowers twisted around the crown. She cocked her head left and right, tucked a few unruly wisps under the floppy brim, and then slipped her purse handle over her arm. Bracing open the screen door with her hip, she maneuvered her empty grocery cart onto the landing, locked the door behind her, and wrestled the buggy down concrete steps to the ground.

Thursday was Specials Day at Glory Mission Thrift Store. She hummed a tune as she pushed her wobbly-wheeled cart along the cracked sidewalk. When she entered the store, a familiar tinkle alerted Miss Annie Hawkins who emerged from the back storage room.

"Miss Lillian. My, don't you look charming. That beautiful red hat was a good bargain last week. Now what can I do for you today?"

"Jus' here a-lookin', Miss Annie. I'll browse around a bit, if you don't mind."

She parked her shopping cart near the counter and wandered among the crowded racks. The store manager disappeared to her sorting and left Miss Lillian to peruse the premises.

By noon, the buggy brimmed with assorted treasures—two purses, a pair of sneakers, three dresses, a crocheted shawl, and another hat. Miss Lillian dinged the bell on the counter. Miss Annie popped out again, rang up her customer's purchases, smoothed the crumpled bills for the register, and thanked her for her business.

Miss Lillian wheeled her bounty up the street, hoisted the loaded cart backwards up the steps, and pulled it through the door. She removed her hat and flopped into her favorite chair.

Whew. These Thursday trips wore her plumb out, but they were worth it. Now every closet was full, every room packed. Soon she'd have enough to see her through until the Good Lord called her home.

Sunday morning she hobbled down the street to Glory Mission Church. Pastor Bertrand Crump welcomed her at the door. "Morning, Sister Lillian. Nice to see you again." He flashed a toothy smile and pumped her hand. "How're you doing?"

She winced. Mister Arthur Itis was kickin' up a storm. "Jus' fine, pastor. And yourself?"

"I'm full of joy, Sister Lillian, full of joy. Praise God, he sent me to this field that's ripe unto the harvest. Come in, come in. We'll sing and shout his glory."

He patted her bony shoulder and then directed his attention to the next in line. Miss Lillian found a seat, dabbed her damp forehead with a lacy handkerchief, and waited for the service to begin. Afterwards, she made her way back to the apartment, shoved aside piles of clothing, and stretched out on the couch.

An hour later, voices startled her.

"Miss Lillian? Are you home? Miss Lillian?"

She rose slowly from her nap, pulled aside dusty curtains, and peeked through the window. Two women stood on the steps. They looked familiar, and she opened the door.

"Hello there, ladies. Won't you come in?"

The tall, blonde woman spoke first. "Miss Lillian, Pastor Bert sent us over to check on you. My name's Christina Matthews, and this is Joyce Henderson." She gestured toward the short, plump woman behind her.

Miss Lillian extended her hand. "Pleased to meet you, Miss Matthews. You too, Miss Henderson. I wasn't expectin' no company, but please have a seat." She swept stacks of newspapers from a nearby chair and dumped them onto the floor. "I'll get another chair from the kitchen."

"No, please don't bother." Christina looked around. "We can't stay long. Pastor Bert asked us to tell you he heard from your housing manager yesterday. The man suggested you might need some help before the inspectors come. We'd like to set a day to return."

Miss Lillian stared at her guests. "Inspectors? I'm not believin' this. You mean Ed Hackett went to Pastor Bert instead of comin' to me? The gutless coward musta known I'd be givin' him a piece of my mind. I don't know nothin' about no inspectors, but there ain't nothin' wrong with my place. Everything's fine. The stove works fine. Plumbin's fine. I don't need no help, thank you. I'm sorry for your trouble."

"Miss Lillian, the authorities will examine all these apartments sometime this week. I think the manager thought you might want to spruce things up a bit. Joyce and I will be glad to help."

"Miss Matthews, you go back and tell Pastor Bert I ain't got no intention of sprucin' things up." She scowled at the intruders. "This place is jus' fine. I don't need no one's help. Now, if you'll excuse me, I'll finish my nap."

The women offered their apologies and hurried away.

Tuesday morning a sharp rap at the door caught Miss Lillian's attention. A young man in a worker's uniform stood with a clipboard in his hand. She opened the door.

"Miss Lillian Lancaster?"

"Yes?"

"My name is Brian Fletcher, Miss Lancaster. I work for Cedar Ridge Health Department, and I'm here to inspect your apartment. Public housing laws require us to make sure all health and safety regulations are being followed. If anything needs attention, the manager will be responsible for correcting the situation within thirty days. May I come in?"

"I s'pose so." She moved aside to let him enter.

Inspector Fletcher stepped into the dimly lit room. He paused, looked around, and then made his way to the kitchen and returned to the front.

"Miss Lancaster, how long have you been living here?"

"Well, let's see. I guess it's been almost twenty years now. Moved here shortly after my Harry died. We had a nice little place out on Kennedy Mountain, but I thought I'd better get me a spot here in town. I don't drive, you see. Harry did all that. Now I can walk wherever I go, unless I call a cab. But that can mount up, you know."

"Miss Lancaster, I see you've accumulated many things, but we're going to have to do something about this. You can't live here under these conditions. This is a fire and safety hazard."

"What do you mean I can't live here? Where would I go?" Miss Lillian's voice quivered with indignation. "I don't have no kids. I have to stay here. This is my home. These are my things. I'm doin' jus' fine, I tell you. Jus' fine."

"You're living in danger, ma'am. If you clean up your place, we won't have a problem. You can stay here as long as you like." The young man hesitated. "Do you have someone who can help you sort through these things and decide what to keep?"

Miss Lillian sank onto the couch. "I'm not sure." Tears stung her eyes.

"I'm sorry, ma'am. I'll get back with the manager. I'm sure you can work it all out. Thirty days. That's plenty of time." He left, and the door banged shut behind him.

The next day Miss Christina and Miss Joyce reappeared on her doorstep. Subdued and sad, Miss Lillian reluctantly accepted their help.

All day she sat in the center of the room, each wrenching decision taking its toll as she mourned the steady loss of her treasures. The women pitched throw-away items into boxes on her right and items to donate into boxes on her left. By the end of the day, only a few precious possessions remained—a photo of Harry in his army uniform; their sweet little Sarah's booties, never worn and still in a box; and some old books that belonged to her mother. Miss Lillian's back ached, her head throbbed, and her stomach twisted in knots. The women left, and exhausted, she fell into bed.

◆ ◆ ◆

Thursday morning, Christina and Joyce returned at nine.

"Miss Lillian, we're back. Are you ready? We should be able to finish today." Hearing no response, they tested the knob. The door was unlocked, and they stepped inside. "Miss Lillian?"

In the bedroom, hazy beams of light filtered through partially drawn curtains. Miss Lillian lay curled on her side under a sheet, her white hair and ashen face a stark contrast to the rosy pink pillowcase. An open prescription bottle stood on the nightstand next to a torn slip of paper.

Christina lifted the note and read the delicate script.

Dear friends,

Thursday is Specials Day at Glory Mission Thrift Store. Please tell Miss Annie I'm sorry, but today I'll get my Glory treasures in Heaven. Thank you most kindly for your help.

Your sister in the Lord,
Lillian Frances Lancaster

Author's note: GLORY TREASURES

The idea for this story originated from comments made in one of our critique groups. A fellow writer talked about an elderly woman who lived down the street from her church. The woman's apartment had become a health hazard, and several ladies offered to help her clean it. However, they had no idea what they bargained for. The woman had accumulated piles and piles of possessions, and she refused to part with any of them.

When my friend spoke about the dilemma the ladies faced, I told her, "That would make a great story." She agreed. However, several years passed, and my friend never produced a story using the anecdote.

In 2008 a Village Writers' Club contest called for a short story featuring "an offbeat character." I thought about that old woman who was such a pack rat, and Miss Lillian Frances Lancaster sprang into being. In December of that year, "Glory Treasures" won second place in the contest.

The Woman in 613

Millie Baldwin peered into the foggy mirror. The second day's sessions would begin in an hour. She'd need to work fast to apply makeup, get dressed, and make it down to the hotel restaurant before eight. With a swipe of the towel, she cleared a spot on the glass and then opened the bathroom door.

No need for privacy. Some of her friends roomed together at the writers' conference, but she preferred to have her own space. Slipping into her underwear, slacks, and blouse, she took another look at her reflection, patted her hair into place, and stepped across the entry to retrieve her sandals from the closet.

From the room next door, distinct sounds permeated the wall—short, quick gasps, a crescendo of guttural moans rising higher and higher—then silence.

Millie blinked fast. The woman's unmistakable orgasm caught her off guard. Embarrassed, she felt like a voyeur peeking into a stranger's bedroom.

Nevertheless, she stood there, straining to hear more. A bed creaking? Low voices? All was quiet now.

Who was this woman making love in the morning? A newlywed with her groom? A young mother with her husband on a weekend retreat? A businessman's mistress with her lover? Perhaps a middle-aged woman with her long-time spouse?

Millie took a deep breath, and tears sprang to her eyes. She and her husband were older now. Ten years ago, she could have been that woman with her spouse.

During their working years, she and Charlie often stole away for romantic weekends. After all their children left home, their empty nest inspired renewed passion, and they spent many happy hours in hotels away from their daily routine. Now in their seventies, they still enjoyed intimate times. But the sound of that woman's full-throated orgasm stirred memories of robust younger years—years when health issues were not a problem.

Millie turned away, picked up her purse and card key, and then stepped out into the hallway. She glanced at the number next door—613. Would she ever see the woman? The conference schedule provided breaks at ten, twelve and three. If Millie returned to her room, she might catch a glimpse of her neighbor.

She was curious, but she would feel awkward if she saw her. As it turned out, she needn't have worried. The woman must have emerged while she was downstairs. Millie never spotted her.

That night back in her room, Millie lounged in an armchair under a lamp. The room next door was quiet, and she pondered the sudden intrusion of her solitude that morning. Strange how that sound from the past had stirred such emotion.

Could she capture her feelings on paper? Maybe she could tell about this in a story. It was a sensitive topic, but readers—especially other women her age—might relate to her experience. She knew she wasn't alone.

Millie pulled out her journal. "Time takes its toll with all of us," she wrote. "Some women lose their lovers to accidents or infirmity, others to divorce or death. Perhaps the lesson here is to make the most of the time we have."

She paused. How thankful she was that she and Charlie had taken time just for each other through all the years.

Then another thought crossed her mind. When their first grandchildren were infants and toddlers, she and Charlie provided surprise gifts to their children. Each note contained an offer to babysit and a check for an "RWG." Her son and her daughter had told her many times how much those "romantic weekend getaways" had meant to them.

She and Charlie could do that again. Their granddaughters, Megan,

Karen, and Katie, were teenagers now, but David and Marilyn and Jennifer and Stan might enjoy new RWGs—maybe now even more than ever. Every couple, no matter how loving, could use a boost.

Millie smiled to herself. She'd discuss it with Charlie as soon as she got home. They might even plan another RWG for themselves.

Author's note: THE WOMAN IN 613

While attending the Arkansas Writers' Conference in June 2010, I spent two nights at the Holiday Inn Presidential in Little Rock. The idea for this story came from a true experience I had on Saturday morning in the hotel. However, due to the sensitive nature of the event, I chose to write the story in third person as fiction, rather than in first person as memoir.

Later that year, I submitted the story to a contest calling for Flash Fiction, a piece containing two hundred fifty to seven hundred fifty words. *Women on Writing*, a popular online magazine, publishes articles and stories written by women, and their quarterly contests have prominent women writers and editors as judges. Winners receive cash awards and have their stories featured on the website.

I received notice that out of three hundred submissions, my entry placed in the top one hundred. It never made it into the top twenty, but I was still happy to know they considered "The Woman in 613" a worthwhile contender.

Priceless

On her way in from the mailbox, Billie Sue shuffled through the day's delivery of bills and junk mail. A long envelope with a handwritten address caught her eye, and she dropped the rest of the pile on the kitchen counter. This might be a personal letter. However, the embossed return address said it was from the White House in Washington, D.C.

Curious, she slid her finger under the flap, tore open the envelope, and slipped out a sheet with White House letterhead. Two lines scrawled in black ink spread across the page:

Billie Sue, thanks for your very kind and inspiring letter. I know times are tough, but knowing there are folks out there like you and your husband gives me confidence that things will keep getting better.
Barack Obama

A letter from the president? Oh, my gosh. Could this really be from *the president*? Billie Sue lifted the paper closer and examined the signature.

Last year she and Michael took the boys to Detroit to hear President Obama speak at one of his town meetings. After she got home, she wrote him a three-page letter and talked about her family's problems. She wanted him to know how she and Michael were faring, despite job losses and her ongoing medical battles:

I don't have a job now. But I do know people are getting them. And I am very grateful my unemployment benefits have been extended. I have returned to college, and my tuition has been covered by a Pell Grant.

Views from an Empty Nest

After she sent it, she wondered if the president even read letters like that from ordinary people. But apparently, he did.

Billie Sue dropped into a chair and reread the handwritten message. Could this really be a reply from the president? Unbelievable.

"Michael, come quick. Look here."

Frowning, her husband stepped in from the den. "What's wrong?"

"No, this is something good. Something great! I just got a letter from President Barack Obama." She waved the paper high in the air and grinned.

"The president?" Michael shook his head. "Nah, can't be. It's just some fake thing made to look like that. You know Obama wouldn't take his time to write a letter to us. Let me see that." Michael reached for the paper.

"No, it's true," she said. "A real letter from President Obama. See there, he talked about the letter I wrote to him." Billie Sue jumped up and gave her husband a hug.

Michael laughed. "Okay, okay. I'll admit it does look legit. Do you think this is really his writing?"

"Sure, it's gotta be. This is so exciting!"

That evening Billie Sue called all her friends. Then she and Michael and the boys ordered in pizza to celebrate, something they hadn't done in a long time.

A few days later, the news about the president's personal letter to Billie Sue appeared in the local paper. She and Michael could hardly walk into Walmart or anywhere else in town without people stopping to talk about it.

The article told how Billie Sue Stofer, the thirty-year-old mother of two boys, nine and six, had been unemployed since 2008 when she lost her job as a lab technician. Soon after that, she was diagnosed and treated for ovarian cancer which was now in remission. Because of her condition, she was ineligible for her husband's insurance, and she had to pay high Cobra premiums. In 2009 her husband, Michael, lost his job too, and their bills were piling up. But Billie Sue's hope-filled letter touched President Obama. She was thrilled to get his response promising "things will get better." The reporter quoted Billie Sue: "Having President Barack Obama think enough about our family's struggles to send a handwritten note to us is a priceless gift—one we will always treasure."

It must have been that quote that grabbed the attention of the autograph dealer in Detroit who contacted her the following week. Even though she said the letter from the president was "priceless," the man made an offer. "I'll give you three thousand dollars for it," he told Billie Sue.

Amazing! Three thousand dollars would go a long way to help pay their bills. But she turned him down and felt proud.

Two months later, the man called again. "An autograph from Obama is worth at least five thousand dollars," he said. "I can write you a check today. What do you say?"

This time Billie Sue paused a little longer. She and Michael had been to nearly fifty interviews since they lost their jobs, and they had filled out hundreds of applications. Her classes at the university were over now, but even with new skills, finding a job seemed next to impossible. Businesses weren't hiring, and her unemployment benefits would expire in six more weeks. Still, she hesitated to sell.

"No, I'm sorry to turn you down, Mr. Jacobson. This letter is not for sale." She clicked off the phone and then second-guessed herself and cried the rest of the afternoon.

Finally, one cold, gray day in November, the dealer called again. She recognized his voice.

"Mrs. Stofer, I know you said you wouldn't sell your memento from the president, but I'm prepared now to offer you ten thousand dollars. I have a client who is willing and ready to purchase it. I hope you will reconsider."

Billie Sue's heart pounded in her throat. She struggled to control her emotions. "That's a very generous offer, Mr. Jacobson. Let me discuss this with my husband, and we'll see."

"Fine. Do you think you could reach a decision by tomorrow?"

"Yes, please call us around noon, and we'll let you know." She clicked off the phone and collapsed onto the couch. Now what? She could hardly wait to talk with Michael. Should they accept it or not? Oh, my gosh. Ten thousand dollars!

That evening after the boys went to bed, she and Michael discussed the offer.

"I don't think we have a choice, Billie Sue," he said. "You know how bad we need the money. That part-time job I have at Henley's isn't worth much. Don't get me wrong. I'm glad I've got it, but ten thousand bucks could sure put us back in the ballgame."

"Yeah, we could pay off most of our bills." Billie Sue gave him a weak smile. "When he calls tomorrow, I'll tell him okay."

The following Saturday, she and Michael dropped the boys at her mother's house and drove to Detroit to deliver the letter to the autograph dealer. In return they received a cashier's check for ten thousand dollars.

Of course, the word got out again, and a follow-up article appeared in the local paper. "I needed to do what's best for our family," Billie Sue told the reporter. "My husband had to practically peel the letter out of my hand, though. I cried halfway there and halfway home. Selling the keepsake was an enormous decision, but I made a copy, and I have no regrets."

After that, things settled down. Billie Sue and Michael used the funds to pay off many of her medical expenses, and that was a relief. Billie Sue landed a part-time job as a receptionist in a nearby clinic, and Michael went back to working regular hours.

On a hot day in August, another strange-looking letter arrived. Opening the envelope, Billie Sue pulled out a familiar piece of stationery—the very same letter she had sold in November. Her hands trembled as she read the short note attached to the page:

Dear Mrs. Stofer,

Last winter, I purchased your letter from Jacobson's Autograph Gallery for $15,000. I was thrilled to have this message from President Barack Obama written in his personal hand.

My collection includes autographs from many celebrities, but this was the first one I ever obtained from a sitting President of the United States. I knew this would appreciate in value; my family could inherit a fortune.

Recently, however, I learned the complete story of where this letter originated. I realized then I would never be at rest until you had this piece back in your possession.

Please accept this now with my sincere admiration for your courage and sacrifice in selling this keepsake to provide for your family. The letter is yours; it was addressed to you. I am extremely pleased to return this priceless treasure to its rightful owner.

Sincerely,
Jonathan Andrew Carlyle

Author's note: PRICELESS

"Priceless" is another fictional story based on an actual event. On November 7, 2010, the *Sentinel-Record* published an article with this headline: "Michigan Mom Sells Handwritten Obama Letter for $7K."

The newspaper story quoted the young, unemployed mother as saying President Barack Obama's kind, personal letter to her was "priceless." However, a persistent autograph collector finally convinced her to sell the hand-written note. "I needed to do what was best for my family," she said, "but my husband had to practically peel the letter out of my hand. I cried halfway there and halfway home."

I used many of the woman's experiences to build my story, but I changed her name and also created a different, happier ending—one I hoped would demonstrate another thoughtful person's "priceless" action.

NONFICTION

The Surprise

"Mama, Mama!" Cathy and I bounded into the campsite where our mother sat reading a book at the picnic table. "Daddy's bringing a surprise."

Mama looked up and gave us a weak smile. She was a city girl, and this kind of family vacation was not what she would have chosen. Roughing it in an army surplus tent for two weeks in the mountains was Daddy's idea. But we were on the last leg of our trip now. This Nebraska campground was only a day's drive from home.

With a big grin on his face, Daddy stepped into the clearing, dragging behind him the largest, meanest-looking snapping turtle we had ever seen. A fishing line was tied to its leg, and puffs of dust billowed as it scuffled across the ground.

"Just look at this fellow," he announced. "I didn't catch any fish, but this old boy will make up for it." He bent down and dangled a stick in front of the turtle's snout. *Crack!* The beast snapped it in two like a pretzel stick.

"Oh, dear."

I could tell Mama wasn't thrilled at all.

"Now just what do you plan to do with that thing?"

Daddy laughed. "Well, I plan to make turtle soup, of course."

"What? You can't do that!"

Mama's angry response surprised me. Then her face scrunched up, and tears filled her eyes.

"Please don't do that. I'm just sick of all this outdoor stuff!" She slumped over the table, hiding her face in her arms.

"Oh, honey, I was only joking." Daddy walked over and patted her on the back. "I just wanted you and the girls to see this friendly fellow."

Poor Mama. She was tired of fighting all the dirt and flies, toting water, bathing in a basin, and cooking on a Coleman stove which had to be pumped vigorously every time it was lit. Daddy's joke about the soup hit a raw nerve.

Cathy and I ran over and patted her too. "It's okay, Mama."

She lifted her head. We grinned at her, and she sighed. A tiny smile flickered.

"You guys are really something, you know that?" She looked up at Daddy. "You just better be sure that old snapper doesn't play a joke on all of *you*!"

Author's note: THE SURPRISE

During the summer of 1948, our family traveled from Kansas City, Missouri, to Colorado on vacation. Tent camping in the Rocky Mountains was a big adventure for my little sister and me. Cathy and I waded in ice-cold streams, collected sparkling quartz, and hiked wooded trails up to mountain meadows with our parents. We even played in patches of snow at the higher elevations.

By the end of the two weeks, though, Mama was tired and ready to get home.

This memoir tells what happened at our last camping spot. I'm not sure why I still remember this so vividly. Perhaps it's because this incident revealed so clearly to me, even as a child, the distinct personality differences in my parents.

The Playhouse

In the late forties, several years after the war, our family moved from Kansas City, Missouri, to Atlanta, Georgia. Cathy and I had no idea what to expect. Daddy spent several weeks down South, looking at houses for sale. When he returned, he brought back several twigs of cotton bolls to acquaint us with this strange, new plant. We took them to school and let everyone finger the seeds still embedded in the soft, fluffy wads.

"This is how it looks before they make it into little cotton balls you see in the store," I told my classmates.

Then, during the Thanksgiving holidays, we were on our way to the Land of Dixie where red clay fields stretched for miles and straggly remnants from picked cotton dotted the landscape.

Highland Terrace, our new street in Atlanta, cascaded down a steep hill, and our house lay at the foot where the pavement leveled before turning right to intersect with the next winding road. Mother laughed and said there was no such thing as "going around the block" in Atlanta. Each street meandered like a stream following the path of least resistance.

While the front of our new house sat on level ground, our back door opened onto a small platform with tall posts supporting it, and we had to descend a long flight of wooden stairs to reach the ground. From there, the yard sloped down in three terraces until it reached a sandy creek bed surrounded by woods. This ravine then stretched a short distance until it met the street behind us, which skirted a neighborhood park.

All these areas were wonderful new places to explore. Cathy and I spent many hours building trails and playing "pioneers" in this surprisingly rural setting right in the middle of the city.

The thing that caught our attention, though, was an old chicken coop. It stood at the bottom of the third terrace with its rough, wooden door opening onto the yard and the rear of the shed up on stilts. A wire mesh pen, also on stilts, extended out above the ravine.

Almost from day one, we began to pester Mother and Daddy to let us turn it into a playhouse. What a great cabin it would be. We could act out our adventure stories inspired by all the Laura Ingalls Wilder books we were reading. Sadly, our parents' consideration for hygiene took precedence over their daughters' imaginations. The old chicken coop was too filthy, they said.

With the advent of warmer days, budding trees, and blossoming flowers, our parents finally gave in to our pleas. Spring cleaning took over, and Daddy helped us scrub down the walls and floors and disinfect cracks so the old coop wouldn't be so grimy. He tore down the wire pen and cut a window into the front of the shed. Mother found old curtains which Cathy and I nailed above the opening and tied back on each side. For days we rounded up orange crates and other old boxes to use for furniture. We were always on the lookout for something that could be transformed into a bed, or table and chairs, or shelves. By summertime, we had it furnished to our satisfaction.

We spent many happy hours in our playhouse. Cooking pioneer meals, we picked weeds for salad, gathered seeds and berries for vegetables, and pressed out mud cakes and pies. Then we poured water into old cups and sipped our imaginary coffee as we talked about our brave husbands who hunted deer or fought with Indians.

Sometimes, we played pioneer school. We'd bring out our dolls to sit on rows of crates as we taught them their ABC's and how to spell and cipher. After creating flash cards from cut-up cardboard, we drilled our students until they could answer without hesitation—nine plus six is fifteen, seven plus nine is sixteen. If one of them made a mistake, we scolded them and sent them to the corner where they faced the wall and wore a dunce cap fashioned from an old newspaper.

I recall we had an ongoing Western drama we played with some of the neighbor kids who lived up the hill. As prospectors, we collected gold dust and stored it in jars inside our hideout. We made this by grinding rocks on concrete slabs until the powder could be scooped up. The dust was pretty colors, and we displayed our glittering jars on shelves inside the cabin.

Then bandits from outside tried to sneak down and steal our gold. We defended our property with make-believe pistols. Hiding until the thieves arrived, we would swoop down and surprise them in the act. Every once in a while, the others came while we were away, and we found some of our precious jars had disappeared. We didn't mind that too much. It gave us an excuse to make more gold.

Sixty years later, I enjoy reminiscing about those days because now I have another "playhouse." My husband and I broke out of our comfortable rut in Mississippi, and like pioneers of old, left friends and family behind to venture out to a new destination. Here in Arkansas, we built a retirement home in Hot Springs Village and settled into this exciting place. Today we sit on our deck and view mountains in the distance, hike wooded walking trails, enjoy beautiful lakes, and play golf on immaculate courses.

Our hideout provides many hours of pleasure, not only for ourselves, but for our children, grandchildren, and friends. Like those youngsters of long ago who romped in and out of that old Atlanta chicken coop, we look forward to many more adventures here in our Arkansas playhouse.

Author's note: THE PLAYHOUSE

The original version of this essay appeared in the *Northeast Mississippi Daily Journal* on November 6, 2001. The newspaper invited readers to submit entries to their "First Person" column. Those pieces could be on any topic of interest to their readers: reflections on what the writer's job meant to him; incidents that gave insight to the writer's life; descriptions of special people or places; or warm memories of families. I was fortunate to have several essays published during the years we lived in Tupelo.

Last year I submitted this revision of the essay to a contest sponsored by Springfield Writers Guild in Springfield, Missouri. On October 23, 2010, "The Playhouse" won second place for Prose: Nostalgia/Reminiscence.

Good Intentions

I watched her enter the classroom. She hesitated, bit her lower lip, and surveyed the other children. With a flip of her hand, she brushed straggly wisps from her eyes and then moved to an empty desk.

As a student teacher, I was nervous too. Noisy youngsters all around me chattered about things third graders find exciting on their first day back to school. With a firm voice, my supervising teacher called the class to order. The room hushed, and the 1958–1959 school year began.

As the weeks passed, I noticed the child was quiet most of the time. She wore wrinkled, dirty clothing more often than not, and other children avoided her. Yet something about this student drew me to her. Perhaps it was her effort to learn. When I worked with a small group, she would be the one most eager to read or answer questions. She seemed to thrive on my attention, and that made me feel proud and useful.

An idea began to form in my mind, and it nagged me for several days before I discussed it with my husband. After our wedding in August, we had moved into a small apartment two blocks from the college and elementary school. Now I was completing my senior year, and he taught in a city seventy miles away. He commuted on weekends and Wednesday nights. Could I work it out with the child's parents to let her spend the night with me on one of the evenings when my husband was gone? My plan included working with her on addition and subtraction and her spelling words. Mostly, I wanted to give her a bath, wash and curl her hair, and treat her as if she were my own little girl. I wouldn't mention that to her parents—only the schoolwork part.

I talked with my supervising teacher, who discussed my idea with the school principal. After receiving his approval, I talked with the child. Her excitement climbed as I thought it would. Since her parents had no phone, I gave her a letter to carry home.

The next morning her eyes sparkled as she handed me the note.

"Momma says I can come home with you if I want to."

At the bottom of the page were only a few words. "It will be all right." I marveled at her parents' trust, happy my plan would fall into place.

Tuesday morning, the child and I talked about how we would walk home together after school. She didn't bring a suitcase, or even a sack with a change of clothes, but I told her not to worry. "We'll make do," I said.

When we arrived at the apartment, I served her milk and cookies. Another child lived across the street, so I let her play outside while I prepared fried chicken and vegetables for supper. During our meal, she gnawed a drumstick down to the bone, reached for another, and then devoured a thigh. Mounds of mashed potatoes and green beans disappeared.

We cleared the dishes and sat on the living room couch to work with flash cards. She cooperated for a while but soon tired, so I didn't push her. Besides, I was ready to begin her transformation.

We drew warm water into the tub and added bubble bath. I gave her privacy so she could undress and climb into the tub. When she was ready, I walked in to check on her. Her thin little body looked small in the tub of bubbles, but her smile beamed.

"This is fun." She slid up and down from one end of the tub to the other. "It's so smooth."

I wondered if her tub at home was rough. Then it dawned on me—she might not even have a tub.

I gave her a washcloth and told her to use the soap and wash all over her body. After several minutes, I helped her clean under her fingernails. Then I wrapped her in a large towel while the tub drained. Her hair needed a shampoo, so we drew more water, and she stepped back in. Now we were both feeling more at ease. Careful not to splash water in her eyes, I laid her back so the warm water surrounded her face. Then I lifted her, applied shampoo, and rinsed it as she lay back in the water.

I toweled her hair and body and then dressed her in a flannel "gown," one of my husband's old shirts with the sleeves rolled up. I combed her hair and rolled it on big brush rollers. She sat in front of the mirror, her eyes wide with expectation as I placed a dryer bonnet over her hair and turned on the heat. When we took down the rollers, her beautiful blonde hair fell in gentle curls around her shoulders.

"It looks nice," she said, grinning from ear to ear.

"I know." I smiled back at her. "In the morning, we may need to put a few rollers in it again before we get ready for school, but it will still look good."

She used a freebie toothbrush from the dentist. Then I tucked her into the makeshift bed of sheets and blankets on the couch. "Goodnight, sweetheart," I told her. "I'm going to get ready for bed now too. See you in the morning." After a hug, she snuggled down.

I gathered her dirty clothes, carried them into the kitchen, and washed everything at the sink. Then I hung her clothes in the bathroom and turned on the heater to dry them. I polished her worn, scuffed sandals. In the morning I would iron her skirt and blouse.

The next day we ate breakfast together, and then we got dressed. I gazed at the clean and happy child in front of me. My little Cinderella was now a princess. I was so eager to take her back to school. She was excited too, and she fairly skipped as we hurried along the sidewalk.

When we entered the classroom, several students were already there. One of the boys looked up. I held my breath.

"Wow! What happened to Carolyn?"

All eyes turned in our direction. She stood there beaming. Before she could answer, another child spoke up. "She went home with Mrs. Young." With head held high, Carolyn walked to her seat.

After school the student teachers had a meeting. As I left the auditorium, I glanced at my watch. Almost four o'clock. A familiar figure bounded from around a corner.

I gasped. "Carolyn! What are you doing here? Did you miss your bus?"

"I want to go home with you again," she said, her face aglow with anticipation.

"Oh, sweetheart. I'm sorry. You can't. My husband is coming home tonight, and besides, your folks haven't said you could."

The smile vanished, and she ducked her head. Frantically, I tried to think. Grasping her hand, I led her to the principal's office. With a heavy heart, I explained our predicament, and he said he would take her home.

Near the campus gate, an old car moved in my direction. I waited while it sputtered to a stop by the curb. An unshaven man, a tired-looking woman, and several blonde-headed children peered out through the open window.

"Are you Carolyn's parents?" I said.

"Yeah. Where is she? She didn't come home on the bus."

He scowled at me. I introduced myself and explained what happened. Then I apologized. "I'm sorry. She should be home by the time you get there."

The man frowned, muttered under his breath, jammed the car in reverse, and headed back the way he had come.

The next day I talked with Carolyn and repeated my explanation of why she wasn't able to come home with me. Her solemn eyes stared back, and she merely nodded. I gave her a hug. "Maybe we can do it again sometime," I said.

I watched her walk away. Her hair was straight, and her clothes—the same ones from yesterday—were wrinkled and dirty.

Blinking hard, I turned and hurried from the room.

Author's note: GOOD INTENTIONS

This memoir has an open ending. Readers often ask me whatever happened to Carolyn. I wish I knew. After I graduated from Northwestern State College in May 1959, Robin and I moved from Natchitoches, Louisiana, to Shreveport. I never saw her again.

I'd like to think Carolyn continued her love of learning, finished high school, and perhaps attended college. Most of all, I hope she developed into a happy, successful adult. It would be fun to meet her again. If she is still living, she would be about sixty-two years old now.

In June 2008 "Good Intentions" won first place in a Village Writers' Club memoir contest. Three years later I read my story on the Arkansas Public Radio show *Tales from the South*.

This weekly thirty-minute program originates at The Starving Artist Café in North Little Rock. Paula Martin Morell, creator and host of the internationally syndicated show, solicits Southern writers to submit true stories. I was excited when she selected my memoir for one of the broadcasts.

On March 8, 2011, Robin and I drove to North Little Rock and enjoyed supper at The Starving Artist that evening with many of our friends. Then I participated in the taping of the show by reading my story in front of a live audience. The program aired on KUAR-FM 89.1 on Thursday, March 24, at 7:00 p.m.

Readers may enjoy listening to the broadcast archived on the show's website: http://www.talesfromthesouth.com

The Perfect Pea

Most folks know about that Peter Piper fellow, pickin' his measly little peck of pickled peppers. Well, let me tell you, that guy can't hold a candle to my Mississippi man.

Last summer my hubby scouted out one of them giant produce operations on a farm about fifty miles down the road. Then he come drivin' in with three heapin' *bushels* full of freshly picked, pink-eyed, purple hull peas. Now that right there was a sight for sore eyes.

He spread 'em out on an old sheet in the middle of the livin' room floor and spent the next three days shellin' every last one of 'em—except for the dry, stringy ones, of course. And he did it all by hand so as not to crush a single pea. No handy-dandy pea-shellin' machine for him, no siree. For days afterwards, he sported them purple thumbs of his like a badge of honor.

Now you folks from Iowa, New York, or California may think you know all about peas since you like to serve them plain little green ones with your heaps of taters all mashed nice and fluffy. But here in the South we're on a first name basis with a whole 'nother family of peas—we call 'em "field peas." We have black-eyeds, crowders, and purple hulls—just to name a few—and the prettiest pea in the bunch is the little *pink-eyed purple hull*.

Them pink-eyes are smaller and lots more tender than regular purple hulls, even the latest "improved" kind. That's why my man never gives up till he finds exactly what he's lookin' for—the old-timey variety he grew up with down on the farm.

I can hear your wheels a-turnin' now, and I bet you're a-thinkin', if this man loves them peas so much, why don't he grow his own, for goodness sake?

Well, if he had the place for 'em, he would. But now that we're retired, we live slap dab in the middle of Arkansas. Our soil is rocky, and the woods all around don't allow much sunshine. So my hubby always checks with his cronies to see where he can buy what we need.

When he finds 'em, he opens a few to see if they're filled out and ready to pick. The secret to good peas is not to wait too late. When they're just right, their long, skinny hulls are sort of a greenish, purplish color, and the little peas inside are green with a pinkish eye. Then he hauls 'em home.

While he's doin' his shellin', the peas fall into a dishpan in his lap, and he drops the empty hulls into a garbage can by his side. Then he stores the shelled peas in plastic gallon bags in the fridge. After that, it's my turn to go to work.

I pour out about a quart at a time, passin' 'em through a couple of rinses to get rid of any sand or trash. After pickin' out the ones with dark, stung places, I pour 'em into a large pot on the stove, cover 'em with water, bring 'em to a boil, and cook 'em uncovered for about three minutes. That seals in the flavor.

Then I pour 'em through a colander, dip 'em in a tub of cold water, then drain 'em again. When the peas are cool, I scoop 'em into plastic pint bags marked with the date and seal 'em tight for the freezer.

When we're ready to eat them tasty tidbits, we cook 'em covered in water with a little salt, seasoned pepper, and a teaspoonful of bacon grease. It takes about an hour to cook up a mess. Then boy, howdy. There's nothin' better than a supper of pink-eyed purple hulls, fresh fried okra, cabbage slaw, sliced homegrown tomatoes, and hot, crusty cornbread. If you want to get real fancy, you can grill some pork chops too, but them peas will always be the star attraction, no matter what else you put on the table.

So, my friends, if you've never sampled this "Southern candy," just give us a holler. We'll be glad to treat you. We guarantee you'll be singin' the praises of them little pink-eyed purple hulls right along with the rest of us.

Y'all come now, you hear? We'll be lookin' for you.

Author's note: THE PERFECT PEA

Each summer my husband, Robin, and I spend many hours shelling and blanching purple hull peas—one of our favorite veggies—to prepare them for the freezer.

One day at the Fitness Center we chatted with friends who had moved from Michigan and told them what we'd been doing.

"We've been puttin' up pink-eyed purple hull peas," I said. Then I laughed. That alliteration sounded so delightful I decided right then to use it in a piece of writing and to tell my story in a distinctly Southern voice.

In December 2009 "The Perfect Pea" won first place in a Village Writers' Club humor contest. The following June, Arkansas Writers' Conference offered cash prizes for entries in a "Food, Glorious Food" literary competition, and the essay won third place.

Borderline

Does life with your spouse seem rather hum-drum—not bad, mind you, but not very exciting, either—just sort of borderline? That's how it was for Robin and me. Then things changed. I guess you could say we each had an "eye-opening" experience.

My husband was due for a colonoscopy. Two days before the procedure, he started that unpleasant cleaning-out process. They say all the preliminary stuff is the worst part. They're right. Neither one of us got much sleep the night before, but we rolled out early Tuesday morning and headed for the hospital.

He felt weak and a little swimmy-headed, but we made it up to the third floor okay. Soon they had us in a private room. He changed into his hospital gown, crawled into bed, and settled back against the pillow. Several folks came in to get his personal information, make copies of his insurance cards, and have him sign papers. They clamped a plastic ID bracelet around his wrist and then started an IV. We waited another thirty minutes before they wheeled him away.

I stayed in the room and read a paperback to pass the time. Later, I strolled down the hall to get coffee. When I returned, the big clock on the wall said 9:32. At 9:45 they rolled him back in.

Robin was really out of it. His eyes were open and glazed over, and his mouth hung open. He looked terrible!

The nurse patted him on his legs and then lifted one of his arms and shook it, but it fell limply back across his stomach. She looked up at me. "What's his first name again?"

"Robin," I said.

She leaned down and hollered into his ear. "Robin! Robin! You can wake up now."

My husband lay there not moving a muscle.

She shook him a little harder. "Robin! It's time to wake up."

I watched to see if he would move. The fluorescent light above the bed cast an eerie glow on his face.

My God, he looks dead!

The nurse reached up and brushed her fingertips across his lids to close his glassy eyes. "Robin!" she shouted into his ear again. Still no response.

"Honey, wake up!" I grabbed his leg through the covers and shook it. He was limp as a dishrag.

The nurse spun around and stepped out to get the blood pressure stand. Then she hooked him up and took a reading. His pressure was normal, and his pulse was fine. But he still wouldn't respond.

An attendant walked in. "We may need to take him back over to the procedure room," she said.

"Please, you need to get him to wake up." Blinking back tears, I moved closer to the bed.

The nurse tried once more. "Robin! Robin! It's time to wake up now." She pounded him hard on his chest and legs.

My husband jerked his head to one side. "Huh?"

"There he is!" She smiled, and I let out a deep breath. "It's wake-up time." Robin struggled to open his eyes.

The nurse continued talking, and he kept dropping off. At least now she was able to startle him enough to keep him coming back.

A few hours later, he managed to get dressed. We were discharged, and I drove us home. He slept like a baby the rest of the afternoon.

The report from the colonoscopy was good. But this little episode has made me do some serious thinking. Seeing my husband lying up there lifeless as a corpse was a shock, but it was a good reminder too. Someday he won't just be sleeping.

Right now both of us are in good health. My husband plays golf three or four times a week. We have our club and church activities. We both like to get together with friends. We still enjoy traveling. Last year, we celebrated our fiftieth anniversary. You know, all of that is way more than borderline. It's great!

I'm thankful Robin isn't the only one who woke up.

Author's note: BORDERLINE

Whenever we Southerners talk about something being a little suspect or not quite up to par, we often say it's "borderline." It was fun to build this essay around that colloquial term.

The incident following Robin's colonoscopy happened a number of years ago, and I wrote this piece soon afterwards. In September 2005 the essay won second place in a White County Creative Writers' contest calling for "A Lesson Learned from Life." Four years later, I updated the piece, submitted it to another WCCW contest sponsored by Central Arkansas Writers, and the essay won third place.

This year Robin and I have celebrated our fifty-third wedding anniversary, and I'm happy to say our life together is still "way more than borderline."

Conversion

Several years ago I had a quiet conversion experience. It wasn't religious—at least, not in the usual sense—but it definitely changed my heart.

In mid-October 2008, my husband, Robin, and I traveled to visit all our children and grandchildren in Tennessee. We spent the first night with our daughter, Sharon, in Franklin. As soon as we arrived, ten-year-old Emily and six-year-old Libbey bounded across the street from a neighbor's house to greet us with hugs. Eddy, our son-in-law, was out of town, but our working-mom daughter had left a roast simmering in the crock pot. When she returned home, we enjoyed a delicious supper.

The next morning I awoke feeling a little woozy but decided to go ahead with my shower. As I washed my hair, my dizziness continued. I thought I might faint, so I sat down in the tub and finished rinsing. Then I crawled out and sat on the toilet with my head down. That didn't help, so I stretched out on the bathroom floor. Finally, Robin came to check on me and led me back to bed.

"This must be a virus," I told him. "I am so mad. We're supposed to have fun with the girls today. This is disgusting."

The morning wore on. Several times I tried to get up, get dressed, and go downstairs for a bite to eat, but I couldn't do it. I even vomited a little, although my stomach felt empty. Emily and Libbey went across the street to play with friends.

At eleven o'clock Robin called Sharon, who is a physical therapist and works at a rehab center. I heard his voice drift up the stairs as he explained the situation.

In a moment he was back in the bedroom. "She said to call nine-one-one; she's on her way."

"Nine-one-one? Honey, *please* don't call nine-one-one. I'm sure this is only a stomach bug. There's no need for an ambulance. See if you can catch Sharon too. She doesn't need to interrupt her day like this."

In spite of my protests, our daughter arrived to take my pulse and check my blood pressure. Both were erratic.

"Okay, Mom. We need to go to the ER. This is how women present when they're having a heart attack." Her medical lingo sounded impressive.

"But I don't have any pain," I said. "How about if I try to eat something first? I still think if I get food on my stomach, this will pass."

She and Robin helped me hobble down the stairs, and I ate toast and drank apple juice at the kitchen table. My queasiness disappeared, although I was still dizzy.

"I'll call my doctor friend and see what he says," Sharon said.

After a brief conversation, she clicked off the phone.

This time *she* was the mother and *I* was the child. "He says you need to go to the hospital and let them run tests. Then you'll know for sure what's going on. With Granddaddy's heart history, you could have some genetic weakness, you know."

Hmmm. I hadn't thought of that. My dad had died with a heart attack.

I looked at Robin, and he nodded. "She's right. We need to check it out."

"Okay, I guess we can go. But not until I brush my teeth and fix my hair. I'm not going anywhere looking like this."

"Mom! I can't believe you!"

"It won't take long."

Before anyone could grab me, I headed up the stairs. My head swam, but Sharon was right behind me.

"Mom! What are you doing?"

"I'm fine. Just let me do my thing. Then we can go."

Stubbornness and vanity prevailed. Sharon checked on our granddaughters who were still with neighbors across the street. Twenty minutes later, my husband and I followed her car to Williamson Medical Center. When we arrived, she and Robin ushered me into the Emergency suite.

An intake nurse examined me. My pulse jumped all over the place—from thirty-eight to one hundred forty, and my blood pressure registered a weak seventy-nine over sixty-eight. I spent the rest of the afternoon in a hospital gown propped up in bed in the ER.

A nurse attached a heart monitor, wrapped a blood pressure cuff around my arm, and placed a clip on my finger. This would keep everyone informed about my vital signs while numerous personnel popped in to ask questions and perform tests—a chest X-ray, EKG, and an ultrasound. They drew blood and set up an IV to administer medicine to regulate my heart.

"You have a little atrial fibrillation going on," a doctor told me. "The upper chambers of your heart are fluttering so blood isn't pumping into the lower chambers the way it should. We want to get your heart back into normal rhythm as soon as possible. A-fib isn't life-threatening, but, if you stay in it too long, clots can form and be thrown out into your blood stream."

At five o'clock Sharon and Robin discussed supper. After my light lunch I was hungry too. Robin made plans to meet Eddy, now home from his business trip. The two men and our granddaughters would have dinner at a favorite Franklin restaurant. Sharon said she would go with them, pick up two take-outs, bring them back to the hospital, and share supper with me. What a sweetheart.

I had no diet restrictions, and an hour later she and I ate our grilled chicken, baked potatoes, and broccoli.

A nurse entered our room. "After you finish, we'll move you upstairs to a regular room. You'll need to stay with us tonight so we can monitor you. If you're still in A-fib in the morning, we'll perform some other procedures to get you converted."

"Converted?"

"That's right. Your heart needs to get back into rhythm."

Soon they helped me into a wheelchair, and I was on my way to the elevator. When I reached my new room, Sharon helped me into bed. A new nurse stopped by to get all my information and set me up for the night.

"You'll be happy to know your heart has converted now," she said. "Our monitors showed it happened in the elevator while you were on your way upstairs. Tomorrow they'll do an echocardiogram, but you won't need to go through those other procedures."

"You mean I'm back in rhythm again? I'm converted?" I grinned at Sharon and the nurse.

"That's right. We'll still keep an eye on you tonight, though."

"Praise the Lord! I'm converted!" I laughed at the play on words. "Let's call Robin and tell him the good news."

My pulse remained steady, and the next afternoon they released me from the hospital. Our son Marty and his family drove over from Maryville, and we all spent a great weekend together.

So that's my "conversion story." Most of us never hear that expression outside of church, but it's fun to tell you about my "change of heart." Now I'm under the care of a cardiologist, taking medication, and doing well. Best of all, I've learned my lesson not to procrastinate. If I ever feel dizzy, I'll get to a doctor right away.

Author's note: CONVERSION

I had never heard the term "conversion" used in any way but religious. So when I learned my heart had "converted," I laughed. What fun it would be to write about this!

My first episode of atrial fibrillation was a complete surprise. I had never experienced any previous problems with my heart. Whenever I went for annual check-ups, my pulse was strong and steady, and my blood pressure readings were excellent. I exercised regularly and was rarely sick. That's why I couldn't believe my distress was anything but a touch of flu.

However, A-fib is tricky and can occur unexpectedly. Doctors are not sure what causes it, although some think stress may play a role.

Now I'm familiar with all the symptoms, and that's a good thing. I won't procrastinate again!

Soft Beds

The smooth cotton sheets felt cool as I stretched my legs and slipped them deeper under the covers. A light blanket lay gently on top of me.

I rolled over and thought of another woman much like me—a wife, a mother, a worker. Earlier in the evening, a television newsman interviewed her husband and grown son as they waited to hear any word about her. Was she dead or alive? She was one of two hundred still missing in the aftermath of the Oklahoma City bombing.

Her husband last saw her the day before when he dropped her off for work in front of the Alfred P. Murrah Federal Building. Thirty-six hours had passed since the explosion demolished most of the nine-story structure. Her family had waited at the site through all those hours—and they still waited.

An earlier news video of two women covered in blood walking from the building had raised their hopes. One of them might be their loved one. But a check of all area hospitals had not located her. Now they were less optimistic.

I worried about the woman. Was she trapped under piles of rubble with heavy chunks of concrete bearing down on her body? I took a deep breath and rolled over again, feeling the light covers slide over me.

Her son had struggled to remain composed while he talked with the interviewer. Then he hung his head, choking back tears. "She was a great mom—and a wonderful grandmother."

Why do these tragedies occur? Why do some human beings do such evil things to other human beings? Why do some of us lie in soft beds while others suffer?

My heart reached out to the other woman, her husband, and her son, and I whispered a prayer for all of us.

Author's note: SOFT BEDS

Writing is often a therapeutic way to release deep feelings of anguish. I wrote "Soft Beds" on April 21, 1995, two days after the Oklahoma City bombing on the morning of April 19.

Until the vicious attacks on September 11, 2001, the Oklahoma bombing was the most destructive act of terrorism that had ever occurred on American soil. The blast claimed 168 lives, including 19 children under the age of six, and injured more than 680 people.

Motivated by his hatred of the federal government, Timothy McVeigh, an American militia–movement sympathizer, detonated an explosive-filled Ryder truck parked in front of the building.

Five years later, on April 19, 2000, the Oklahoma City National Memorial was dedicated on the site of the Murrah Federal Building, commemorating the victims of the bombing.

Deliver Us from Evil

When violence stretches out its ugly hand and strikes someone we love, it is always a shock. For some reason, we are never prepared to deal with it, even though newspapers are full of it, television programs dramatize it, and movies entertain us with it. Yet the reality of violence invading our personal worlds never occurs to us. We think we are immune—or maybe we just hope we are. Then the nightmare comes true.

♦ ♦ ♦

Friday morning the telephone rang at seven o'clock. We are retired now, so calls that early are unusual.

The bathroom door opened, and Robin stuck in his head.

"That was Jan. Marilyn called, and they think Leesa, Wanda's daughter, was abducted last night. She was on her way home from working at Comer's and had a flat tire. They found her car abandoned, and they're still searching for her."

My mind reeled, trying to make sense of what I just heard. Leesa Gray, the teenage daughter of our niece Wanda Farris, worked at the family restaurant established by Robin's sister Joyce and her husband, James Comer, now both deceased. Everyone in the little community of Dorsey, Mississippi, loved Comer's. The food was great, and the people were friendly. How could she have been abducted right there in Dorsey? That was crazy.

I climbed out of the tub and dressed. As Robin and I ate breakfast, we talked some more.

"Is there any possibility she might be at a friend's house?" I asked.

"I don't think so. They found all her personal belongings still in the car—her keys, her purse. It doesn't look good."

J. D., my brother-in-law, drove to the restaurant. He returned with an emotional story. The sheriff and other law enforcement officers had combed the woods and surrounding area all night. They had a suspect in mind—a man in his thirties who was from the Dorsey area. After graduating from high school, he left to join the marines and was now a recruiter based in Vicksburg.

The fellow was in the restaurant the day before, hanging around and talking with the young women. Before closing time, he ordered two cheeseburgers to go and then left right after Leesa. When the officers went out to his grandmother's house, they left an officer there to watch his van while they went to get a search warrant. In the meantime, the man said he was "going fishing," and he took off into the woods.

Later that morning the officers returned, confiscated the locked van, loaded it onto a trailer, and transported it to the Highway Patrol Investigative Office in New Albany. There they began a slow, meticulous search inside the van for evidence.

All day crowds of friends and family members gathered at Comer's, keeping prayer vigils going round the clock. Law officers continued to search for Leesa and also for the man. We talked with our grown children and other friends and asked for their prayers.

Friday evening we received the call. Leesa was dead. The investigative team found her body inside the van. When they worked their way to the rear, they discovered her body under the fold-down seats. No one else was allowed to see or touch the remains. The state medical examiner in Jackson would be the one who would perform the autopsy.

My stomach churned. I felt weak. How could this happen to Leesa? Why would anyone single out such a sweet, innocent person? It didn't make sense. My head throbbed, and my heart ached for Wanda, her husband Mike, and all the family.

The man was in custody. Officers and their dogs had tracked him down, and earlier that evening, they had picked him up along another country road. He was being held in an undisclosed location.

Saturday and Sunday was a blur. We shed many tears with the family and received condolences from friends at home and at First Presbyterian Church in Tupelo. Monday night we attended the visitation at the funeral home. Tuesday morning the memorial service was held at the local high school gymnasium.

Leesa was a vibrant, beautiful young woman, a leader of her junior class and active with her youth group at Bethel Baptist Church in Dorsey. Hundreds of her young friends turned out to hug her mother and cry on each other's shoulders.

♦ ♦ ♦

Why did this happen? There are no good answers. Human actions and laws of nature often create tragedies which cause us to suffer. Only through the loving care of family and friends can we find our way through the anger and the grief.

The Bible says our Heavenly Father will not leave us desolate and in despair. In the Second Letter of Paul to the Corinthians, Chapter 1, verses 3–4, we read, "Blessed be the God and Father of our Lord Jesus Christ, the Father of mercies and God of all comfort, who comforts us in all our affliction, so that we may be able to comfort those who are in any affliction with the comfort with which we ourselves are comforted by God."

We cling to that promise, trusting His love will overcome even the most gruesome circumstances. "Deliver us from evil," we pray. "Deliver us from *evil.*"

So be it, Lord, so be it.

Author's note: DELIVER US FROM EVIL

For victims of violent crimes and their families, the healing process is long and difficult. Two years after Leesa's death, her mother, Wanda Farris, was interviewed by a staff writer for the *Northeast Mississippi Daily Journal*.

"We always talk about her," Wanda told the reporter. "We laugh about the things she used to say or the things she did. She's gone from our sight but not our hearts." A photo in the newspaper showed Wanda displaying a quilt made from her daughter's T-shirts and those given to her by Leesa's classmates and friends.

Our great-niece Leesa Marie Gray was killed on June 23, 2000, less than a month before her seventeenth birthday. Marine recruiter Eddie Loden, thirty-six, pleaded guilty to her murder in September 2001 and was sentenced to death. He remains on Death Row in a Mississippi prison.

When I wrote this piece after Leesa's death, I wasn't sure if our family would ever fully recover from this tragedy. However, eleven years have passed now, and we have seen how God's great love can work to overcome evil.

On September 2, 2006, "Deliver Us from Evil" won second place in a White County Creative Writers' contest calling for a spiritual or inspirational essay.

My Life with a Loving Atheist

How can an atheist and a Christian live happily together? How can they find true joy and fulfillment in their marriage?

I'm sure many of my friends have wanted to ask me these personal questions but have been reluctant to probe. I want to assure them a close relationship between two diverse thinkers is not only possible, it can actually thrive. Love and respect for each other is the foundation.

Perhaps I should begin by clarifying the term "atheist." Many people think an atheist is a person who vehemently declares, "There is no God." Unfortunately, some atheists do make dogmatic statements like that, but they are expressing an idea that goes beyond the strict definition of "atheist."

A "theist" is a person who believes in a god or gods, and an "a-theist" is a person *without belief* in a god.

Why is my husband Robin an atheist? He sees no compelling evidence for a god, no proof of any supernatural being or force beyond the universe. However, he refrains from declaring such an entity does not exist. He simply says, "According to the evidence I have at this time, I do not believe there is a god."

On the other hand, I can say, "I do believe there is a god." The magnificence and complexity of the universe leads me to believe there is an intelligent source for all that exists. As a Christian, I also believe this source is a loving being whose power and grace are revealed in the life, death, and resurrection of Jesus Christ. However, I know my beliefs cannot be proven. I accept them on faith.

Often, angry Christians will stand up to atheists and declare, "Yes, there is a god." In my opinion, these Christians overstep their human boundaries as much as angry atheists who say, "No, there is no god." The truth is, none of us can say for sure if there is a god or not. We Christians *believe* there is a god.

With this understanding comes respect for those with whom we disagree. I cannot always be right, and you cannot always be wrong. We are all finite human beings, limited in what we can know about anything beyond our world.

How did my husband come to his way of thinking?

Robin grew up in a Christian home. His parents were Methodists, and the family attended a small country church. When I met him in college during the fifties, he was a strong believer, often leading Bible studies and discussions at the Wesley Foundation. I attended Westminster Fellowship, the Presbyterian campus ministry, and during our courtship, we were active in both youth groups. Friends called us "Mesbyterians." We were married in a Presbyterian church by a Presbyterian minister.

Throughout the early years of our marriage and while rearing our three children, Robin and I attended Presbyterian (USA) churches. He served as a deacon and also taught Sunday school, often moderating adult discussion groups. His experience as a public school teacher and principal, as well as his years as an administrator in a regional mental health center, equipped him to facilitate friendly exchanges where Christians could express their doubts openly without fear. His extensive study of the Bible, church history, religion, and philosophy grounded him well.

However, Robin has always been an avid reader and a searcher. As he moved into later adulthood, he wrestled more and more with the basic tenets of Christianity. One day he realized he could no longer honestly say he believed in the divinity of Jesus. Even his belief in God, as portrayed in the Bible, diminished. The Bible was no longer the Word of God for him. He saw the many books of the Bible as written by human beings from their human perspectives, steeped in the culture of their time, full of scientific and historical inaccuracies and many inconsistencies. Why did the Christian church insist that the Bible was Scripture, a holy book to guide us in our daily lives? This didn't make sense to him.

Even so, Robin believed in a supernatural entity for a time, a god that did not intervene in history or human affairs. Finally, he gave up that view as well.

My husband and I do not argue about our ideas. He knows I am committed to Jesus Christ and believe God's Spirit can speak through the Bible. He recognizes I am where I need to be at this time, and he understands why I believe.

I know he has come to his position because he is a free thinker who is committed to reason and logic. I often think of the story of Thomas in the Gospel of John. This disciple of Jesus needed concrete evidence before he could believe.

My husband is a loving humanitarian, willing to help our neighbors or whoever is in need. He serves his Unitarian Universalist fellowship in many ways, often leading Insight programs. Our children adore him for his calm, steady approach to life and life's problems, and his grandchildren delight in his attention. He is at peace with himself and others.

I thank God every day for my husband, Robin.

Author's note: MY LIFE WITH A LOVING ATHEIST

Before we moved to Hot Springs Village, Arkansas, Robin and I were active members of First Presbyterian Church in Tupelo, Mississippi. However, as time passed, he became more and more uncomfortable "playing the role of a believer," as he put it. He had been asked numerous times to serve as an elder on the Session, the ruling body of our church, but he always refused.

Our first summer in the Village, we attended Presbyterian Kirk in the Pines. The pastors and members welcomed us with open arms. However, in September Robin finally said he'd have to follow another path. He couldn't continue to worship with me.

At first it seemed strange—and sad—not to have him by my side, but I understood and respected his decision. I joined the Kirk, and Robin became a member of the Unitarian Universalist Village Church. We are each happy now, and he has found another loving fellowship in which he can openly express his views.

On September 4, 2010, "My Life with a Loving Atheist" won third place in a White County Creative Writers' contest, the CMH Inspirational Award.

A Thanksgiving to Remember

"Over the river and through the woods, to Grandmother's house we go."

True to the words of that old song, our family often gathers for Thanksgiving at "Grandmother's house" here in Arkansas. But sometimes, my husband and I are the ones who travel over the river to celebrate the holiday in our children's homes. This is the story of a Thanksgiving in Tennessee we will always remember.

In late September 2008, our older son, Steve, and his wife, Tonya, journeyed from Franklin, Tennessee, to Kazakhstan in Central Asia for the final two months of a lengthy and tedious international adoption. If all went as planned, they would return to America on Thanksgiving Day with a precious bundle in their arms—their own baby daughter, Lily Grace. After years of worry and waiting, what a blessing that would be!

The day before Thanksgiving, Robin and I headed to Franklin and arrived at our daughter Sharon's house a little past four. Earlier in the day, our son Marty and his family arrived from Maryville, Tennessee, and he and his wife, Anna, took their daughter, Audrey, and our other two granddaughters, Emily and Libbey, shopping in Nashville. When we entered the house, the girls rushed to give us a hug and then proudly displayed a cute Build-a-Bear teddy they purchased for their new little cousin. Embedded in the toy was a recorded message. Each girl said a line: "Welcome home, Lily Grace. We love you. From your cousins, Audrey, Emily, and Libbey." When we squeezed the teddy bear's hand, their voices sounded loud and clear. Lily Grace would love it.

Wednesday evening Robin and I treated everyone to supper at a nearby restaurant. Then we drove to Steve and Tonya's house and spent the night in their guest bedroom—a strange feeling with no one else there except Lucy the cat. However, the young woman who had been their house sitter left everything clean and fresh, and we slept well.

Thursday morning I prepared a large spaghetti casserole and salad for lunch—a different kind of Thanksgiving dinner, to be sure—but we planned to have our turkey on Saturday after Steve, Tonya, and Lily Grace adjusted to the time change and rested from their long flight. Marty, Sharon, and their families came over, and Sharon and Anna decorated the house with pink tulle and balloons to welcome home the world travelers. Our granddaughters drew three large Welcome Home posters, which we hung on the back entry, the nursery door, and the mantel.

At four o'clock we piled into cars and headed for the Nashville airport. On Thanksgiving Day, freeway traffic was light. We arrived, parked, and entered the large terminal about a quarter to five.

Our children's e-mails said they were due about five thirty. We checked the display board for their flight number, happy to see their plane was on time. After layovers in Frankfurt, Germany, and Chicago, they were scheduled to arrive from O'Hare at five twenty.

We settled down but decided to go across the way to a small restaurant in another part of the terminal for a cup of coffee. It's a good thing we did. Over there we ran into Tonya's dad, Ron, and his three sons. Ron had learned they would enter through Gate A, not Gate C.

Finally, the display board indicated their plane was on the ground. Soon passengers began to trickle up the concourse and through the gate. Bubbling with excitement, Audrey, Emily, and Libbey waved helium balloons high in the air: "Welcome Home," "Welcome Back," "Welcome Baby." People smiled as they moved past, but there was no sign of our threesome. When the pilots walked through, we began to worry. Did they miss their flight?

Then we spotted them. "Here they come!"

Grinning from ear to ear, Steve and Tonya approached us with wide-eyed Lily Grace in her mother's arms. Cousins shouted. Cameras flashed. Aunt Sharon, Aunt Anna, and Grandmother Maddie laughed and cried. Granddaddies Ron and Robin beamed with pride.

I threw open my arms. "Welcome home, sweethearts. We thought we'd missed you."

"Lily Grace was asleep," Steve said, "so we waited to be the last ones off the plane. But here she is, everybody!"

Lily Grace took us all in, fixing her gaze on each one with a solemn look of bewilderment. Who were all these crazy folks? Quiet and calm, she let each of us hold her as she searched our teary, smiling eyes.

How beautiful she was. Her chubby cheeks and rosebud mouth reminded me of the Gerber baby, only this child of the world had dark, almond eyes. And what a little chunk. My ten-month-old granddaughter felt solid and comfortable in my arms.

Uncle Eddy retrieved their luggage from the baggage carousels downstairs, and soon we headed for the parking lot. Now another first was about to happen. Experienced daddies Marty and Eddy carefully strapped Lily Grace into her new car seat. This time she whimpered, but Tonya climbed into the back seat next to her, and everything was better. New daddy Steve collapsed into the front passenger seat, thankful to have Eddy chauffeur them home.

Home! What a wonderful word!

Robin's seventy-sixth birthday fell on Thanksgiving Day that year, but we waited until Saturday to celebrate. He opened his cards, and we cut the cake, but the radiant smiles on his *four* granddaughters' faces were the best gifts of all.

Author's note: A THANKSGIVING TO REMEMBER

In November 2010 a contest sponsored by the Maumelle Arts Council called for "Memoir—an event that made a lasting impression in your life." This account of our first meeting with Lily Grace won second place.

Lily Grace is now three years old. She and Sam, her new baby brother from Kazakhstan, are the two youngest grandchildren in our family. What a blessing they have been for Steve and Tonya and for all of us!

Uncle Sam Greets Little Sam

Hello, there, little fellow. I see you've arrived in America now. That journey from Kazakhstan last week was long and tiring—scary for you too. Your daddy, Steve, tells me you cried almost the whole trip. But your mommy, Tonya, and sister, Lily Grace, waited for you at the Nashville airport, and you quieted down when you saw your Sissy. You reached out your little hand to her, and she beamed with pride. "He likes me," she said, and you smiled. I'm sure that moment was only the beginning of many happy years for the two of you together here in your new land.

You and your three-year-old sister are natives of Kazakhstan, a large country in central Asia whose people are proud of their rich cultural heritage going back thousands of years. However, during much of the last century, Kazakhstan was part of the Union of Soviet Socialist Republics. If you had been born under communism, you and Lily Grace would have grown up with many limitations on your freedoms. Recently, Kazakhstan regained its independence, and now it is well on its way to becoming a vital, prosperous country once again. But here in America you will enjoy even more blessings than in the land of your birth. Your mommy and daddy have adopted you, and you are now citizens of the United States of America, the greatest land of opportunity in the world.

Every person in America is free to learn and work and pursue whatever kind of life he would like, as long as he does not interfere with another's rights in doing this. As a result, Americans enjoy a standard of living envied by millions. You and Lily Grace will grow up in a loving, middle-class, well educated family who will nurture you and provide you with whatever you need to become happy, healthy, successful adults.

We Americans are people who come from many different backgrounds so you will be welcome here. We are not all the same race or the same religion, and we do not think alike. But we respect one another, and we guarantee equal rights for all our citizens, rich or poor, young or old, male or female.

We treasure our privilege to vote in free elections and choose our leaders. And we abide by the laws our leaders establish. If we don't like the laws, we work to have them changed. We do this by demonstrating in nonviolent ways, talking with our representatives, and urging our elected officials to listen to the will of the people. Our government is for the people and by the people. We will not allow a dictator or any authoritarian group to run our country or tell us what to do.

Americans believe one of our basic human rights is to choose our own religion. Your mommy and daddy are Christians, and they believe God was with them and with you as they ventured over to Kazakhstan to meet you in the baby house and go through the legal process of becoming your parents. In your native land, many people are Muslims, but now Kazakhs enjoy religious freedom too, and like us, they can practice their religion in a progressive and tolerant society.

In the United States, we uphold the separation of church and state. Our government and public institutions cannot force citizens to pray or worship any god, nor can the government prevent the free exercise of religion when it does not harm others or coerce others to conform to a certain religious practice. Our people worship in a variety of churches, synagogues, temples, and mosques, and our government refrains from favoring any one religion over another.

Soon you and your sister will begin school. Lily Grace already goes to preschool, but she will attend public school when she is five years old. In America, we have established free public education, kindergarten through twelfth grade, for all children in our land. Parents may pay to send their children to private schools, but all our citizens support our public schools with taxes, and we elect representatives to oversee them.

Educators encourage citizens and parents to become involved to make sure all children are learning and reaching their potentials. Your grandmother and granddaddy were public school teachers and administrators, so they will have a special interest in your education. They know that you and every other child in America will be our nation's future parents, workers, and leaders. This land of freedom that we love will be in your hands.

So, little Sam, you have many exciting days ahead. Your family loves you, and your Uncle Sam will always support your right to be all that you can be. Welcome to America, Samuel Ethan Young. Your future is bright!

Author's note: UNCLE SAM GREETS LITTLE SAM

Early in 2011 our son Steve and his wife, Tonya, spent six weeks in Kazakhstan, going through the process to adopt their second child, Samuel Ethan Young. While they were away, our son Marty and his wife, Anna, cared for Lily Grace in their home in Maryville, Tennessee.

In mid-February Steve and Tonya returned home for a joyful reunion with Lily Grace. Six weeks later they received word the paperwork in Kazakhstan was completed, and Steve flew back to Kazakhstan to pick up Sam and bring him to America.

Soon after their arrival, I noticed a contest sponsored by the 2011 Arkansas Writers' Conference entitled Grand Conference Award II: A Reminder to Americans. Guidelines called for an essay, one thousand-word limit, reminding us of values and other blessings worth keeping. I thought of all the benefits Sam would enjoy in his new home, and I wrote and submitted my entry. What a thrill it was when "Uncle Sam Greets Little Sam" won first place!

On Thursday, June 30, 2011, a few days before Independence Day, the *Williamson Herald* in Franklin, Tennessee, published the essay along with a family photo of Steve, Tonya, Lily Grace, and Sam. His parents have clipped the column as a keepsake. One day our grandson will be able to read this patriotic account written by his Maddie, telling him all about his arrival in America.